The Evolution of
DR. STEVE PRATT

The Evolution of
DR. STEVE PRATT

Heidi A. Wimmer

authorHOUSE®

AuthorHouse™
1663 Liberty Drive
Bloomington, IN 47403
www.authorhouse.com
Phone: 1-800-839-8640

First published by AuthorHouse   01/23/2012

ISBN: 978-1-4685-4706-1 (sc)
ISBN: 978-1-4685-4705-4 (hc)
ISBN: 978-1-4685-4704-7 (ebk)

Library of Congress Control Number: 2012901364

Printed in the United States of America

CONTENTS

CHAPTER 1

This book centers on Dr. Steve Pratt, who is the head of the Emergency Department at Bay County Hospital. The hospital is small but a powerful beacon to the surrounding community.

The head of the hospital is Dr. John Dobinson, who is the figure head of the hospital. The third member of this dynamic team is Dr. Dave Bradfield, who is head thoracic surgeon and director of medicine. Dr. Dave Bradfield is Dr. Pratt's boss, and through the years they have become friends, doing much for each other.

For example, one of Steve's friends from college, Dr. Wayne Moore, asked if Steve would consider a new job as head of the hospital in York, which would be an advancement in Steve's medical career. Dr. Moore was getting ready to accept a partnership in his fiancée's father's practice and thought Steve would make an excellent replacement.

When Dr. Moore called, it couldn't have come at a worse time because Dr. Bradfield was suffering through the unexpected loss of his wife, trying to keep him and his two children afloat. How could his best friend think of leaving now?

This was causing a great deal of mental anguish for Steve because he was thinking about putting his career before his best friend. Through many sleepless nights, Steve made lists of why this move was good; yet, he kept coming back to the fact that Dave was going through such a rough time that he couldn't abandon him. After all, Dave had done so much for him over the years.

The decision was continuing to take a real toll, both mentally and physically, on Steve. The doorbell rang and Steve knew that it was Dave because he had invited Dave over he had come to a decision. Dave hadn't seen him in a couple of days, and in those couple of days Steve hadn't eaten much and certainly hadn't slept much, and he looked like hell.

Steve opened the door, and Dave was shocked to see what kind of condition he was in. Dave asked as he sat down, "Are you okay? You look like hell!"

"I'll be okay soon. I apologize for looking like this, but this decision has been difficult both physically and mentally for me, but I have come to a decision, and I wanted you to hear it from me first," said Steve in a low voice.

"Whatever you decide will be okay with me."

Steve smiled at Dave, and Steve took a deep breath and said, "My decision is to stay at Bay County. I'm not ready to run a hospital on my own."

"Are you sure about your decision?"

Steve said with a smile, "Yes. I want to be here at Bay County; in fact, I've always wanted to be here."

The next day at work Steve worked with a renewed vigor that had all of his co-workers buzzing and at the end of the shift he gathered most of his co-workers around and told them what had been going on and his decision to stay at Bay County. Everybody cheered and patted him on the back.

Then at shift's end he got on the phone and called Dr. Wayne Moore at York and explained to him what his decision was. It was hard telling Wayne, but he understood, and Steve told him that he would see him at the wedding. Wayne agreed, and they both hung up the phone. Steve took a deep breath and was glad that was over. Now he could give his full attention to the emergency room at Bay County.

For the first time in a few days Steve ended up getting a restful night's sleep, and the next morning his appetite came back as well. It would soon become clear to him why he made the decision to stay.

Steve was in the ER waiting for blood work to come back on a sixty-two-year-old female who was complaining of numbness and tingling in her right arm, severe jaw pain, and a stiff neck. Immediately

Steve asked the patient if she had any history of heart problems and that scared the patient and she wanted to know if she was having a heart attack. Steve calmed her and continued to ask questions about her medical history. He gave her an aspirin and patched her into an EKG machine or an electrocardiogram, which records the heart's electrical activity, and ran a quick strip. There was some elevation in her T-waves, but nothing that indicated a heart attack. Steve said to the woman, "I'm going to draw some blood and run a cardiac enzyme test and then we'll know more soon."

The patient seemed to understand. As Steve walked out of the exam room he gave orders to one of his nurses to draw labs for a cardiac enzyme test on the patient in exam room two. The nurse took the chart that Steve was holding, went to the medical cabinet, and got all the necessary equipment that she would need to get the blood tests done.

Steve was just about to check the board for his next patient when an explosion shook the floor that he was standing on. Steve at first couldn't figure out what happened, and then he thought radiology was directly beneath the ER. That was where he headed first. He ran for the stairs and went down them. As he approached the next floor down Steve could smell burnt plastic. As he went into radiology he could see several technicians frantically running around. Steve stopped one of them who had a look of a deer in the headlights and asked him, "What happened?"

The technician replied, catching his breath, "I think one of the x-ray machines blew up. There was a workman here just earlier this morning working on that very machine."

"Show me where," asked Steve in a huff.

The technician led him to a small interior room that now had its faux walls in pieces. Steve looked concerned at the mess before him and said, "Do you know if there was anybody in the room when the machine blew?"

"No. I don't know, but I can help you look," said the technician.

They both stepped over large pieces of the machine and started moving pieces of wall. The technician yelled at Steve, "Over here, Dr. Pratt. I found somebody!"

Just as Steve looked up at the technician, he also found somebody in the rubble. Steve said to the technician, "Get all the debris off him, but don't move him. I've also found somebody."

Steve moved pieces from the partition wall off the person who was currently laying face-down. As he finished moving all the debris, Steve knelt down and felt for a pulse. There was no pulse. Then he slowly and with great care rolled the deceased person over and came to the horrible conclusion that the deceased was Sam Neal. He'd been a radiology technician for a number of years. Steve lowered his head in sadness. The technician who found the other person had cleared all the debris from him and brought Steve back to reality. He yelled at Steve, "Dr. Pratt, this person is alive. Come quick!"

Steve stepped over pieces of partition and parts of the x-ray machine. This person was also on his stomach, and Steve felt for a pulse. It was strong and regular. Steve gave direction to the technician, and they turned the person onto his back. Steve looked and looked again and to his disbelief, but before he could process what he saw the technician asked, "Isn't that Dr. Bradfield?"

Steve couldn't speak at that moment, but he nodded slowly. Steve looked widely around and saw a gurney that looked undisturbed from the explosion and said to the technician, "Get that gurney over here, so we can get Dave onto it and get him up to the ER."

The technician did as he was told, and between the two of them they got Dave's unconscious body on the gurney and wheeled him to the elevators. Steve said to the technician, "Good work. You need to call the morgue to come and get Sam Neal, then you need to follow me up to the ER with a portable x-ray machine that won't explode."

The technician once again understood his directions and followed them to the letter.

Once in the elevator, Steve started to assess Dave's condition. Steve didn't have time to freak out; he just acted instinctively. Once back in the ER, Steve grabbed Connie, his head nurse, and they wheeled Dave into trauma room one. Steve gave Dave a quick head to toe. Steve put a C-collar on Dave because of the trauma to his head, face, and neck area. That was the area where most of the injuries were confined to.

Dave had some major lacerations on his face, probably some facial fractures, which he would confirm with the x-rays. The technician who helped him down in x-ray brought up the portable x-ray machine. But before Steve could tell him what pictures he wanted, Dave went into respiratory arrest. Quickly Steve inserted a breathing tube into Dave's airway, and Connie started to bag him. Connie, who was Steve's number one nurse. At first he was hard to bag, then the bagging became easier, and that elevated his respiratory arrest. He was then hooked up to the ventilator and his breathing stabilized.

Steve said to Connie, "Go and call Dr. Dobinson and tell him what happened and that he needs to help out down here until Titus is free."

Dr. Dobinson, who is head of the hospital and is not use to getting his hands messy, but the tone of Connie's voice, told Dr. John Dobinson that she was serious. Titus, who is an orthopedic surgeon by trade but doubles as everything that is needed, was in surgery with a young up and coming football player who had totally trashed his knee. Connie understood, stepped out of the trauma room, and made the phone call.

John immediately came down to the ER and checked in on Steve and Dave. Steve asked him, "Could you pick up the slack until Titus gets out of surgery?"

The nurses helped John get acclimated to the ER, and shortly he was seeing patients and treating, then streeting, most of the patients he saw.

Steve was now ready for the technician to take the pictures, and Steve told him what series he wanted. After the technician was finished, Steve came back into the trauma room and the films were already down loaded to the computer in the room. Steve quickly looked at them and realized that his injuries were even more extensive than he first thought.

The x-rays showed that he had a fractured left orbit, fractured left clavicle, fractured nose, and four broken ribs all on the left side. There was no doubt about it; Dave was going to need an orthopedic surgeon. Just as Steve was calling up to the OR to see if Titus was finished with the football star's knee, he appeared in the trauma room. Steve put the phone down and was glad to see him. Titus went over to the computer, looked at the x-rays, and said, "Wow, what a mess. Are you ready for me to take him up to the OR?"

"Almost. Let me start a couple of IV's, then there's the issue with his breathing. He went into respiratory arrest and I had to tube him and put him on the vent."

Titus took his stethoscope and listened to his lungs, then took the stethoscope and put it back around his neck and said, "Sounds like maybe one of his broken ribs nicked a lung. I'll take care of that once he's on the table."

Titus who was an excellent surgeon, but he also knew that he was good, but in his own way he was also sort of a nerd. Dave and Steve usually just tolerated him, but in this case Steve was counting on Titus to fix Dave. Titus left to get scrubbed for surgery, and Steve said to the orderlies, "Take Dave up to OR three."

After they wheeled Dave out of the trauma room, Steve came unraveled. He sat on the floor and started to shake uncontrollably, then broke down and cried.

Then his thoughts went quickly to Dave's kids, so he pulled himself together the best he could at that moment, called Lydia, and explained what happened and what was happening now. She wasn't sure what she should do. Steve calmed her and said to her, "Bring the kids up after school and I will explain what happened to their father."

Lydia, who is the live in nanny that was hired shortly after Dave's wife passed, understood and would bring the kids just as soon as school was out. Now not only did Steve have to worry about Dave, but he now was going to have to tell his fragile kids, who not too long ago lost their mother, that their father had been hurt in an x-ray machine explosion.

He thought this was the reason why he stayed, to help Dave. During the time he was waiting for Dave to come out of surgery, he called John and checked on his patient who was having the heart related symptoms. John said, "She has been admitted to medicine and currently tests are being run and a stress test is going to be performed in the morning."

Steve understood and asked John to keep him up to date on that patient. John told him that he would, and he also wanted to know about Dave as soon as he knew something about the outcome of his surgery. Steve understood and hung up the phone.

Considering how extensive Dave's fractures were, Titus was in surgery with him for almost four hours. About halfway through that time Lydia showed up with the kids. J.J. looked worried, and Sam was just excited to see Steve. Steve stood and approached the kids and immediately tried to put his best not worried face on. Steve gave Sam a big bear hug with sound effects, which was a typical Uncle Steve greeting since she was small. J.J. asked, "What happened to dad, Uncle Steve?"

Steve sat down and all four of them sat in sort of a huddle and Steve said, "Your dad was standing nearby an x-ray machine that malfunctioned and exploded. Dr. Titus is in the OR fixing his injuries and he should be fine."

"How does an x-ray machine explode?"

Steve put on a brave smile and said, "That's the question we all are asking."

All four of them sat in relative silence until Titus came out of the OR. They all stood and Titus approached. He sat down, then they all sat with him. Titus said, "Man, you both have grown up, I almost didn't recognize you J. J.. You're turning into quite the handsome young man, and you, young lady, you're the spitting image of your mother."

"How is my dad," J.J. asked forcefully?

Titus was taken back some, but didn't let that bother him, and he said, "Your dad will be sore for a few days, but I put all of his broken bones back together again. He should be in a regular room in another hour or so."

J.J. said in a normal tone of voice, "Thank you very much, Dr. Titus, for helping my dad."

Titus stood and bowed to J.J. and replied, "My pleasure, young Bradfield."

Steve smiled at Titus, and Titus smiled back. Steve wanted so much to be with Dave in recovery, but thought that Dave's kids needed him more out in the waiting room. About an hour had passed since Titus had come out and told them that Dave was going to be okay when Steve got a text from Titus. All the text said was, "911 Recovery."

Steve read the message and, without alarming, anybody got up and said, "I'll be right back. I'm going to see what room they're moving your dad to."

Steve went into the recovery room and saw Dave thrashing about. Steve got right up by his bedside and put a hand on Dave's shoulder. Titus took the tube out of Dave's throat and reestablished oxygen. Dave was blinking his eyes open, then closed, then opened again. Steve asked, "What's wrong?"

Dave said in a whimper, "I can't see! I can't see!"

Then he sobbed. Steve gripped his uninjured shoulder and asked, "Can you see anything?"

"No. Are my kids here? They can't see me like this; it's too much for them this soon after Kelly's death. Please, Steve, make sure they don't know."

Dave was grasping with his one good arm and hand at Steve. Steve grabbed that hand and held it tight and said, "Don't worry about anything I'll take care of making sure your kids are okay."

Steve turned to Titus, who was still in the room, and as Steve was calming Dave down, Titus ordered a CT scan. Titus asked, "Do you want me to sedate him and put the breathing tube back down?"

That calmed Dave somewhat. His breathing was becoming labored at best, and Steve put a re-breather mask on him, turned the oxygen flow up to six liters, and that seemed to help.

"I can't see, I'm not deaf; talk to me. I still can make medical decisions for myself."

Titus walked over to Dave and said, "Look, you're on six liters by mask now and you can't keep your saturation levels above seventy. You're scheduled to go to CT soon. If I don't tube you before you go, you'll never make it through the scan. Then I'll have to pull you out of the scan and tube you anyway."

Dave got angry and said in short breathless bursts, "You don't know my saturation levels may come up and my breathing may even out."

Titus rolled his eyes, and then said, "Yeah, when pigs fly."

Titus got a call from radiology, and they were ready for Dave's CT scan. Titus, with the help of an orderly, wheeled Dave to radiology. Steve went back out to the waiting room and sat between Sam and J.J. Steve said, "I talked with your dad and he told me that it was late and both of you should be home in bed. He wasn't feeling very good after his surgery, so I gave him some medication to help him sleep, and that's what he wanted you both to do. After school tomorrow you should be able to see him."

Both children were disappointed but believed their uncle Steve, and they went home with Lydia. Steve sighed big and just hoped that he wasn't lying to them that they could see him tomorrow after school.

Steve hustled down to radiology and found Titus waiting for the results. He sat there with his arms folded in front of him, and he looked pissed. Steve didn't want to ask, but did anyway, "What's the matter?"

"I had to tube that stubborn man that you call a friend in there," replied Titus in a huff.

"Have the scans come back yet?"

"No, I'm hoping to hear anytime now."

"Are you thinking subdural hematoma that's pressing on or close to the optic nerve?"

Titus nodded slowly. Just then a young radiology technician came out and said, "Doctors, your CT scan is complete, and the views are cued up in room two."

Both doctors got up quickly and walked into room two. They both got right up close to the images, then Titus said, "Look here Steve."

Titus pointed to a small dark blob close to Dave's optic nerve. They were both right about their diagnosis. Titus said, "This is delicate work we're talking about. This is way out of my comfort level."

Both men were quiet, then Steve said, "Dr. Sands is a surgical ophthalmologist, I've never worked with him, but he is said to be tops in his field."

Titus agreed and called Dr. Sands. As luck would have it, he was still at the hospital. He even answered his own phone. Steve filled him in, and Dr. Sands said to Steve, "Let's not waste time. Is Dave strong enough for surgery now?"

"Yes, I believe so. He was having some breathing issues earlier, but he's intubated and breathing better now."

"Since I don't have my regular team, can you both scrub in and bring the CT scans? I'll meet you in OR three in five minutes."

"What about anesthesia?"

"I just saw Dr. Cooper a couple of minutes ago giving a spinal injection to some pregnant lady. I'll track him down and meet in room three."

Dr. Sands and Dr. Cooper were already scrubbed when Titus and Steve brought Dave into the OR. Dr. Cooper made Dave ready for the operation. Dr. Sands took the CT scan views and studied them carefully while Steve and Titus scrubbed. Once everybody was in the OR, Dr. Sands said, "According to the CT, it looks like Dr. Bradfield has a hematoma near or on his optic nerve. Does everyone agree?"

Both Steve and Titus agreed, then Dr. Sands said, "Okay, Dr. Cooper, put him under. I'm going to go in through his sinus cavity which will be less invasive than cutting into his forehead."

Once again both Steve and Titus agreed. Then Dr. Cooper said, "Okay, Dr. Sands, he's ready for you to begin."

Steve and Titus stepped closer to the table and assisted Dr. Sands in removing the hematoma. Both doctors were impressed with the skill and expertise in which Dr. Sands operated. As Dr. Sands packed Dave's nose, he said, "Dr. Bradfield will have some pain for a few days, and his eye-sight will be blurry, but should return to normal within a day or two."

Both Steve and Titus thanked him. They walked out of the OR feeling pretty good about the situation, then Steve got a page. Steve immediately recognized the number. It was John. Steve grabbed his cell phone out of his pocket and dialed John's number. John answered on the first ring. John asked, "How is Dave?"

"He's out of surgery, but not awake yet, so we're not sure, but Dr. Sands seems confident. What do you need," asked Steve?

John asked, "The patient you saw in the ER who was complaining of jaw and arm pain, her stress test was normal. We've done every test that I can think of, and her heart isn't the cause. Her pain in her jaw is extreme and has remained constant, but her arm pain has gone away. I'm at my wit's ends. Do you have any suggestions?"

Steve thought for a moment and remembered back to when she first came into the ER and when she showed him where the pain was. At the time he didn't think much of it and, together with her other symptoms and also her age and weight, Steve quickly jumped to heart-related and never even looked in her mouth. Steve asked John, "Are you with the patient now?"

"No, but I'm just outside her room."

"Go back into her room and look at her mouth. See if there's evidence of teeth grinding. I'll wait."

Steve could hear John walk back to her room and asked her to open her mouth. Then a few moments later John said excited, "Yes, she definitely has evidence of grinding her teeth."

Then the light bulb went on and he said to Steve, "You're thinking Temporomandibular Joint?"

Steve smiled on the other end of the phone and said, "Great job, John. Nothing gets by you."

John replied also with a smile, "Hey, now I'm just a little rusty on some things, but give me time and the right prompts and I'll eventually get there."

Steve couldn't help to laugh directly in the phone. Dave asked, "We've been giving her pain medication, but now I know the diagnosis. I should add an anti-inflammatory drug and a muscle relaxer, right?"

"Very good. You need to get out of your office more often. You might tell her that most dentists make appliances for TMJ. You might write a script for one just in case. As soon as you get her pain under control, she can be discharged whenever you see fit to do so," replied Steve.

"Okay. She'll be relieved that we now have a diagnosis that doesn't involve her dying."

Steve pushed the end call button on his phone, turned his attention to Dave, and waited for him to come out of the anesthesia. Steve sat next to Dave and reflected on the woman whom John had been treated and was glad that everything was going to be okay.

It was early that next morning and Dave was just starting to come around. Steve stood next to Dave's bedside and Steve watched in anticipation for Dave to blink, then he blinked again. Dave quickly became agitated and spoke up, "Anybody there?"

Steve grabbed his uninjured hand and held it. Dave said frantically, "Steve, I thought Dr. Sands got the hematoma with no complications. I can't see!"

Steve couldn't believe what he was hearing. Dr. Sands seemed so sure about his procedure. "No light or shadows?"

Dave, almost hysterical, said, "No, nothing. First Kelly dies on me, now I'm blind, how, who, is going to help my kids!"

Steve quickly injected something into Dave's IV, and Dave quickly fell asleep. He didn't want to, but he felt he had no other choice but to sedate Dave.

Steve had to get his emotions under control before he went to find Dr. Sands and figure out what the hell was going on. Steve took a couple of deep breaths and stormed off to Dr. Sands' office. Steve didn't even knock before he entered. He opened the door abruptly, and Dr. Sands was shocked, but also could tell that something was wrong. Dr. Sands, getting up from behind his desk, asked, "What's wrong?"

Steve paused for a moment to collect himself, then said, "Dave woke up and he couldn't see. He got so agitated that I had to sedate him."

Then Steve turned and left his office, and Dr. Sands followed Steve back to Dave's room. Even though Dave was out, he was still agitated, tossing and turning. Dr. Sands looked at Steve and said, "I need him conscious for the exam."

So Steve gave a small amount of epinephrine to Dave, which brought him to a conscious state within just a couple of minutes. Dr. Sands asked Dave, "Dave, its' Dr. Sands. Can you see anything?"

"No, why can't I see? I thought you removed the hematoma?"

"That's what I'm going to try and find out. Hang in there I'm going to examine you now."

Dr. Sands' examination of the eye showed the eye to be clear, but he would need another CT to see if he missed something, and that wasn't an easy topic for Dr. Sands to handle.

Both Steve and Dr. Sands waited anxiously for the scan to be finished. Then, with the radiologist still in the room, both Steve and Dr. Sands looked at the images as they were being produced. Both doctors pointed to a small dot, which looked like a pin prick on the images. "It looks like there's a small piece of the hematoma that had moved away from the original mass, and that piece must still be putting pressure on Dave's optic nerve," said Dr. Sands.

"When do you want to go back into surgery," asked Steve?

"Right now, if possible. I don't want that optic nerve to tear, then it truly will be the end of Dave's sight."

Steve wanted so badly to say why this wasn't taken care of the first time, so instead he physically just walked away from Dr. Sands and would wait in the waiting room until he was out of surgery for the second time. Two long hours later Dr. Sands came out of the OR, approached Steve, and said, "It took longer than I thought because there was a small bone obstructing the piece of hematoma which I had to remove dangerously close to his optic nerve. Unfortunately I couldn't go through his sinus cavity for this surgery. I had to make an incision just above his right eyebrow, and I don't believe it should leave a scar."

"What about his sight," asked Steve?

"We'll have to wait until he regains consciousness."

Dr. Sands then went back into the operating room. That left Steve in the waiting room all by himself, and he was overcome by emotions. He said as he began to cry, "Please, God, I know I haven't talked to you in a long time, but please don't hold that against Dave. If you could, please allow Dave to see again, we're all still fragile after Kelly's death. Amen."

Steve continued to cry quietly. Then something startled Steve. He looked at his watch and it was almost three. Dave's kids would be here soon expecting to see their dad and have their dad see them. Steve quickly called Lydia and explained what was going on. He told her to do something to stall the kids until she heard back from him. Lydia told him that it wasn't going to be easy, but she would do her best. Steve pushed the end button on his phone and breathed a sigh of relief. He wiped his face off, got his emotions in check, and went into the recovery room. There he waited and waited until Dave started to come out of the anesthesia. Dave blinked, then blinked several more times quickly. He looked around the room, then centered on Steve, who hesitantly asked, "Can you see?"

"It's blurry, but I can see you, and what a sight for sore eyes you are, literally," Dave said happily.

Steve was crying, and so was Dave. Steve once again brought himself under control and called Lydia, Dave smiled as the tears streamed down his face. Steve told Lydia that she could now bring the kids. Lydia was relieved that Dave was going to be okay. Shortly after Steve talked to

Lydia, Dave was moved to a regular room, and Steve helped Dave looked presentable for his kids.

The hospital smock covered his clavicle and shoulder injuries, but he couldn't undo the heavy bandage from his most recent surgery and the killer headache that went with his recovery. Then the door opened wide to his room, and both J.J. and Sam rushed in and hugged Dave tightly, which caused pain to run through his body. He grimaced, but didn't let his children know that he was in pain. Steve quickly grabbed Sam, who was lying on his broken clavicle, and pulled her away and sat her next to Dave by his side. Dave breathed a small sigh of relief and J.J. asked, "Are you okay?"

"I will be now; you don't know how good you both look to me right now. I love you both so much!"

Sam said, "We love you, too daddy. I've been waiting all day to see you. It was sure a long day!"

Both Steve and Dave looked at each other and laughed at Sam's remark. The happy reunion went on a few more minutes before a nurse came in and told everybody it was time to let the patient rest. They all did as they were told, even Steve. Dave asked, "Hey, Steve, can you wait a minute?"

The nurse objected, but Steve reassured her that he would only be a minute. The nurse held up one finger, and Steve nodded. Steve then went back inside to Dave's bedside and Dave said, "I know that I had told you it would be your decision whether or not you took that job in York and that my friendship with you shouldn't be a consideration. I know that's what you wrestled with the most, and I just want to thank you for considering our friendship. I thank God that you're in my life and my children's lives every day."

"Get some rest. You are going to need it. We'll all be back tomorrow after school."

Dave smiled and Steve left his room. The nurse went in and administered his pain medication, and Dave slept through the night.

Dave spent three more days in the hospital, each filled with visits from his kids and Lydia. He was then released from the hospital with only a small bandage over his right eyebrow and a sling for his shoulder.

As Dave recovered at home, he came to realize just how much he missed Kelly and how alone he seemed to be, especially during the day when everybody was at school. Everywhere he turned reminded him of a memory, some good and some not so good.

CHAPTER 2

On the day before Dave was to come back to work, he got up and knew something was different about this day, then he realized that today would have been Kelly's birthday. Today was harder, and Dave tried not to show any outward emotion, but it was a tough sell. Lydia realized that something was wrong and asked him about it after the kids had gone to school. She asked, "Dave are you okay? Should I get you something or call Dr. Pratt?"

"No, Lydia, it's just that today is Kelly's birthday, and I miss her so much."

He went upstairs, and Lydia didn't see him again until that afternoon when the kids returned home from school. He looked awful, as if he'd been crying all day, which he had. As the kids came home, Dave put up a brave front. It fooled Sam, but J.J. knew that it was Kelly's birthday. He didn't want to upset Sam, so he, too, kept his emotions under wraps; like father, like son.

That evening when Dave thought both of his children were in bed, J.J. knocked softly on Dave's bedroom door. Dave wiped away the tears quickly, cleared his voice, and softly said, "Come in."

J.J. entered his room, got to the foot of Dave's bed, and came unglued. He started to cry and shake. Dave quickly flew out of his bed and comforted his shaken son. Dave said in a whisper, "I know, J.J. that today was hard. It was hard for me as well."

J.J. replied in what seemed to be such a small voice, "Dad, I miss mom so much, and today was her birthday."

J.J. continued to cry, and Dave cried along with him. Finally J.J. cried himself to sleep, and Dave just left him sleeping next to him in his bed. Dave watched J.J. sleep and thought how alone he really was and how much he missed Kelly. She was truly his soul mate. The night passed slowly, and it turned out to be another sleepless night for Dave, which of late he had had several.

The next morning was a normal routine for the Bradfield household, except for Dave. Dave once again put on a brave front for his kids and Lydia. Once the kids were off to school and Lydia had left for classes at the local community college, Dave let his guard down. He still couldn't shake the deepest loneliness that he had ever felt. He didn't feel this way at the funeral or even on the day that Kelly died. Dave couldn't understand why he was feeling this way now. He didn't even think he could get it together enough to go to work and until now work had been therapeutic for him. Dave pulled himself together long enough to make a phone call to Steve. Steve picked up his cell on the second ring and asked, "Dave, what can I do for you today?"

Dave shook his head on the other end of his phone and said, "You're so weird. I'm really not feeling well this morning. I don't have anything pressing; can you cover for me?"

Steve, more serious now, replied, "Is it your head, your shoulder? Do you need an antibiotic?"

Dave replied, "No, not sick like that. I do need you to write me a script for a sleep-aid, and I think I need an antidepressant."

Steve asked, "When did it get that bad? Is it because of your recent medical problems?"

Dave replied, "No, I'm fine physically, and it's never been this bad. It was Kelly's birthday yesterday, and it's been like somebody turned on the faucet. I can't figure out how to turn it off. I haven't been this upset even on the day Kelly died. Can you help me out?"

"I'll help you, but I'd like you to see a therapist," said Steve.

"Yeah I'll see a therapist, but let me get my emotions in check before I make an appointment. Man, it is weird hearing sound advice coming from you. It has been such the other way around for so long that I'm just not used to you sounding so, for lack of a better word, authoritative," replied Dave.

"I learned it all from you, I've heard this coming from you, and I just assumed some of it rubbed off. I'll call the prescriptions in to your local pharmacy. You should have them in an hour or so. I'll check with you later."

After Steve hung up with Dave, he called in the scripts to Dave's local pharmacy. He called a low dose of an antidepressant and a sleep-aid that was just a little stronger than that's offered over the counter. He didn't want Dave to become dependent on either of the two drugs he had prescribed.

Once Dave got the medication, he started taking the medication as it was directed on the label and, with the help of the sleep-aid, by the next morning he was able to function well enough to get back to work.

Steve was glad to see him back at work, and Steve checked in on Dave and wondered how things were going. Dave told him that thus far the medication was working and that he need not worry because he made an appointment with Dr. Lena Douglas for the end of the week. Steve was actually proud of him and said, "Wow, I never honestly thought you would have made an appointment."

Dave sheepishly responded, "I confess, if it weren't for my kids I wouldn't have made an appointment so quickly."

Steve understood, but was glad anyway.

Dave was in his office when he called Steve in the ER and told him what was happening. Dave told him that he was starting to experience anaphylaxis.

Steve grabbed a couple epinephrine pens from the medical cart and ran up the stairs to Dave's office. Steve, on his way to Dave's office, yelled at a nearby nurse as he ran past her and told her to bring a gurney to Dave's office. She didn't hesitate and did as she was told. Steve rushed into Dave's office and was stopped cold in his tracks by what he saw. Dave was unconscious with his head tilted back against his chair, and he was turning blue around his mouth and lips. His fingertips were also turning blue. Steve quickly moved toward him, felt for a pulse. There was one; it was slow, but palpable. Steve jabbed the epinephrine pen into Dave's thigh, and moments later Dave took a large gasping breath.

Steve monitored his pulse and blood pressure. The nurse brought the gurney, and between Steve and the nurse they managed to get Dave loaded onto the gurney. They rolled him into a nearby treatment room. Steve started him on oxygen and also started an IV with normal saline and gave Dave more epinephrine and waited to see how he would respond before he did something more invasive like activated charcoal.

The large amount of epinephrine made Dave more conscious, and the bluish color around his mouth and fingertips was starting to go away. "Man, you gave me a scare; I didn't know you were allergic to the antidepressant."

"Neither did I. How would I have known? I've never taken a drug like that before. Damn! Do you know how much that epinephrine pen hurts when you jab it into my thigh?"

"Sorry, but yes, I do know what it feels like, but it's still the best drug I know to help relieve the symptoms of anaphylaxis rapidly."

"Thanks for your help; it seems that lately I've been saying that a lot to you."

"It's good to hear it from you, because usually the roles are reversed and you're saving my bacon."

"I'm feeling much better. Can I get up now?"

Steve had his reservations, but helped Dave up. He felt so light-headed and dizzy that he quickly lay back down. Steve quickly took his blood pressure and it was low, but as he laid there for a while, his blood pressure normalized. "Does that answer your question?"

Throughout the next twenty minutes Dave continued to try and get up off the gurney. Finally he managed to get to a sitting position, then, with the help of Steve, managed to stand up. At first he was shaky, then he regained his balance. Steve had a concerned look, and before he could say anything, Dave said, "Don't worry, I'm going home. Lydia is there this afternoon and evening."

Steve still had a concerned look, and Dave added, "Really, Steve, I'm okay. I'm going home and going to bed."

Steve told him that he'd call him and check on him later. Dave called Lydia and told her that he was coming home because he wasn't feeling well and that she would have to pick up the kids from school. She understood, but was also concerned for his welfare.

Dave made it home. He was shaky and unstable at best on his feet. That was a side effect of the epinephrine; he also had a major headache that also was a side effect. Once home, Lydia helped Dave upstairs and into bed. Once Dave was settled, Lydia told him that she was going to the market, then picking the children up from school. She wanted to make sure Dave was going to be okay by himself. Dave reassured her and thanked her for getting him settled. Lydia left his room, and Dave fell asleep almost immediately.

When Lydia and the children returned home, Lydia had instructed the kids not to disturb their father because he wasn't feeling well. They both understood and did what they were told.

Lydia made dinner, then went upstairs to Dave's room. She knocked, but there was no response, so she entered the room. She tried to wake him and couldn't raise him. This scared her. She went back downstairs, and in her calmest manner fed the kids then went back upstairs and tried again to wake him up. Lydia was panicked. She used the phone in the bedroom and quickly called Steve's cell phone. Steve picked it up immediately because he saw it was Dave's home number. "How are you doing, Dave?"

"Dr. Pratt, this is Lydia. I'm not sure what to do, but I can't get Dr. B to wake up."

Steve asked, "Is he breathing?"

Lydia replied in a shaky, panicked voice, "Yes, he's breathing. He looks normal, just like he's sleeping, but I can't get him to wake up. I'm scared."

Lydia started to cry, and Steve said quickly, "Okay, Lydia, calm down. I'll be there soon."

Steve grabbed his medical bag, got hold of Titus, then flew out the hospital doors. He made record time in getting to Dave's house. Lydia opened the door and softly said to him, "The children don't know about Dave's condition. All they know is that he wasn't feeling well."

Steve understood and quickly ran up the stairs. J.J. and Sam wanted to know why Steve was here. Lydia reassured them that their daddy was sick and Steve was here to check on him. They understood and went back to what they were doing.

Once upstairs, Steve quickly checked Dave's vital signs and they were all normal. The abnormality was that his temperature was slightly elevated. Steve snapped an ammonia capsule and waved it closely under Dave's nose. There was no response. Steve wasn't sure if all this was due to the reaction from the anti-depressant or the amount of epinephrine given to him to counteract the anaphylaxis. He was frustrated. He quickly went back downstairs, took Lydia aside, and told her, "I can't get him to respond, and I don't want to guess. I want him in the hospital. I don't want the kids to freak out when the ambulance comes, so if you could help me shelter them somewhat I'll explain to them what's going on."

Steve and Lydia went into the family room and gathered both kids together. "How is our dad?"

Steve looking directly at J.J. and replied, "He had a reaction to a medication, and he's sick. I want him to go to the hospital so I can make him better, but to get him there safely the ambulance needs to come and take him to the hospital."

Both children understood and J.J. said to Steve, "Please make him better, Uncle Steve, because we'll have no parents if you don't."

Steve gathered both of them and hugged them tightly, then Steve said through silent tears, "Don't worry, I won't let anything bad happen to your dad. I promise!"

He pulled away from them both, and Lydia whisked them away into the den where they wouldn't see their dad being brought downstairs unconscious on a gurney. Steve made the call to 911.

The ambulance came, and the EMT's went upstairs on Steve's orders and brought Dave downstairs on a gurney. They took him right into the ambulance. Steve told Lydia that he would call her when he knew something about his condition, then he rode with Dave in the ambulance to Bay County.

The ambulance ride was uneventful. Dave's vital signs remained normal. Once in the ER, Steve directed the EMT's to put Dave in a treatment room. Once in the treatment room, Steve ran a full blood count and toxicology screen. Steve continued to monitor him closely, but there was no change. All remained normal except for the fact that he wasn't regaining consciousness. Steve also ordered a magnetic resonance imaging (MRI) and a positron emission tomography (PET) scan looking for any abnormal brain activity. Steve had thought that maybe he had slipped into a coma. The PET scan would show an abnormal reading if Dave was in a coma.

The blood work came back essentially normal besides the concentrated levels of epinephrine, which was understandable. Then Steve waited for the MRI and the PET scan to be completed. Finally the results came back. The MRI was normal, but the PET scan showed some abnormalities. It showed that Dave was in a low state of coma.

So now Steve had to work backwards to see what had been causing the coma. Was it the anti-depressants, or was it the reaction to that medication or was it the anaphylaxis or some combination of all three? Steve did more tests and came to the conclusion that it was a combination of the anti-depressants and strain of the anaphylaxis reaction causing his coma.

Steve gave Dave medication to clear his system of both the anti-depressants and the epinephrine. Then Dave was transferred to a private room in the ICU. Steve quickly called Lydia and filled her in on Dave's condition. Lydia wanted to know what she should tell the children. Steve recommended just telling them that Uncle Steve was still trying to make their daddy well, and it would take a few days. Lydia understood and would tell them what Steve had told her to say. Steve also told Titus, and Titus told Steve not to worry about his ER, that he would look out for it until he came back. Steve was glad to hear that. Now he could just concentrate on Dave's condition. Steve sat by Dave's bedside waiting for him to regain consciousness.

On the fourth day of Steve sitting at Dave's bedside there were signs of Dave starting to come out of the coma. As that day progressed, Dave became fully conscious. Steve was right there when Dave opened his eyes and asked hoarsely, "What happened?"

Steve patting him on the shoulder, replied, "You lapsed into a coma. This is the fourth day."

"Are my kids okay?"

"They're fine. Lydia has been taking great care of them. All they know is that you've been sick and had to stay in the hospital."

Dave's voice still raspy asked, "What caused all this?"

Steve, scratching his head said, "My best guess is that it was a combination of the anti-depressants and the epinephrine. I gave you drugs to help flush both the anti-depressants and the epinephrine from your system, then I hoped it would be just a matter of time before you regained consciousness, and it was. You're sure hard on your fellow doctors."

Dave looked over at Steve and said, "You do look pretty bad. You should take better care of yourself."

Both Dave and Steve laughed.

Dave remained another day in the ICU just as a precaution, then he was moved to a regular room. He was in a regular room for another three days, where he could have visitors, and his kids were glad to see him and know that he was going to be okay. After the third day it was hard to keep Dave in bed and away from his office, so Steve did the next best thing; he discharged him. Steve gave him specific orders not to step foot in the hospital for a week. He made sure his orders were going to be followed. He told Lydia, and Lydia reassured Steve that his orders would be followed if she had to tie him down. After she said that, she turned bright red, and Steve was amused at that and got a good laugh. Finally Lydia had to laugh as well.

Then Steve got serious with Lydia for a moment and asked, "You love him, don't you?"

Again she turned that same shade of red and replied, "This must stay between you and me, and it can never get out. Yes, I love him very much. These last few weeks when he was so sick I wasn't sure how I could have gone on without him. It's not just him, Steve; I love his kids as if they were my own."

"How can you live under the same roof with Dave and not share these feelings with him?"

Lydia, with tears welling in her eyes, replied, "I'll share my feelings with Dave when he acts on his feelings first, and until then I'll be nothing but professional when it comes to my emotions and Dave. I'll love his children unconditionally regardless of my feelings for Dave."

She quickly wiped her eyes, gathered the last balloons out of his room, and followed the nurse, Dave in the wheelchair, with his kids on either side of the wheelchair.

The week that Dave was banished from the hospital seemed to fly by, but there were certain things that got accomplished. The basement got reorganized and cleaned out, and so did the garage. By the end of the week Dave was feeling good about getting those things completed and Lydia was sad to see him go back to work.

As Dave went back to work, it was business as usual at the Bradfield house except for Lydia's feelings for Dave.

CHAPTER 3

Day in and day out Lydia had to fight with her emotions. It was beginning to wear on her both physically and emotionally. One night at dinner Sam asked Lydia, "You don't look good. Fix Lydia, Daddy!"

Dave stood and approached Lydia as she was seated at the table. She tried to talk him down and away, but Sam insisted. Dave felt her forehead and took her pulse, and both seemed okay. Lydia quickly rose from her seat at the table and said, "Thank you, Sam, for your concern, and yours also, Dr. B, but I'm fine, just my school work is getting the better of me, too many late nights and early mornings."

Dave, sitting back down at the table, asked, "Anything I can help you with?"

Lydia buried the thought that popped into her head and said, "Not unless you want to help me with advance calculus and chemistry two."

"Why would you take both of those classes in the same semester?"

"I'm wondering that myself."

"You go study the kids and I'll clean up. I'll get the kids up and off to school in the morning. You can either sleep in or study. Either way, I don't want you to feel like you can't come to me and ask for a little time away from being the Bradfield's slave. I don't want to lose you; you're way too valuable to this family."

Lydia smiled, thanked him, and went to her room. She shut the door, sat on her bed, and had a huge melt down. She cried and cried, and when she thought she couldn't cry anymore, she continued to cry. Then, from her room, she heard a dish break, and before she could wipe her face she quickly ran out into the kitchen. Dave was bent down on the floor picking up pieces of a broken plate. The kids were in the den doing homework. Lydia bent down and immediately helped him gather pieces from the broken plate. When he stopped and looked at her, she was red-faced, and her face was tear-streaked. He also noticed that her hands were shaking as she was picking up the broken pieces of the plate off the floor. Dave grabbed her hands, pulled her gently to a standing position, and they were face to face. Dave said quietly, "There's something wrong."

"No, there's nothing wrong," replied Lydia.

"Then tell me why you've been crying and your hands are trembling."

Lydia wanted to tell him exactly what was wrong, but feared the worst and quickly said instead, "I found out that I flunked my chemistry two lab, and I'll have to do that lab again if I want to pass the class."

Of course that wasn't true; in fact, she was proud that she had a B average in that class. Dave accepted that story and asked, "Can I get you a tutor for that class?"

Lydia forced a half smile and said, "No, Dr. B, in the first place I can do this myself and, if I can't do it myself, then I need to stop and go in a different direction, because I know that it's only going to get harder from here. I appreciate the offer, but no thank you."

Lydia went back into her room, shut the door, stood there on the other side of the door, took a deep breath, and said to herself, "Lydia, your emotions almost got you caught. You need to get a hold of yourself!"

Lydia grabbed her cell phone and called Steve, the only person who could help her with this problem. Steve answered on the second ring. "Pratt, speak."

"Dr. Pratt, this is Lydia."

"Is everything okay? You sound upset."

"You remember what our conversation was about the other day? Well, I'm currently struggling with my emotions. I was in my room crying and a plate dropped in the kitchen. Anyway, he noticed that I'd been crying, so I made up a quick story about failing a lab test at school.

I don't know how much longer I can go on like this." She sobbed into the phone.

"Okay, take a breath and try to calm down. I've been in this position before. I helped Kelly do the very same thing you want me to do for you several years ago. Trust me, Lydia, I won't give your secret away, but I'll try to make him see you not only as the Bradfield's live-in maid, but as a woman who has feelings for him."

Lydia was scared by what Steve said and she said, "I don't know about this. Maybe these feelings will go away if I suppress them long enough."

"All that will do is make you sick. Can I ask you a personal question?"

Lydia hesitated and said, "I guess so."

"How many relationships have you been in?"

Lydia again hesitated, then replied, "I'm not sure where you're going with this, but I've only been in one committed relationship."

"How did that end?"

Lydia really not wanting to answer him did anyway, "The relationship lasted a year and a half, then his unit got called to Iraq. Shortly after he got there, his unit was attacked and he was killed."

Steve was shocked and was sorry that he brought it up, but said in reply, "I'm sorry, Lydia. I hate to see anyone suffer emotionally, so please let me help you. I promise that I'll be careful."

After a long pause Lydia said, "Okay, but you can't make me lose this position."

"Don't worry, Lydia, and if you don't call me Steve, I'll be forced to hurt you!"

Lydia managed a small laugh and replied, "Okay, Steve. Thank you for helping me."

"That's what friends are for."

Both of them hung up the phone.

The next day Dave came back to work and everybody was glad to see him back, which included his secretary Rose. Steve stopped by that morning and welcomed Dave back. Dave was glad to see Steve and wanted to know if anything new or exciting happened while he was gone. "You make it sound like you were gone for such a long time.

Nothing out of the ordinary happened. Bay County is still the same. How was everything at home?"

"It was good. I got the basement and the garage cleaned out. Lydia has been a great help to me. She pitched in and helped a lot. I'm so glad that she's now a live-in."

"I think she's great as well. We visited when you were in the hospital. Just curious; there's nothing between you two, is there?"

Dave looked down at his desk, then back at Steve, and said, "I think one day I'd like there to be, but for me it's too soon. I still miss Kelly so much."

Steve, trying hard to hide his disappointment said, "You're going to always miss Kelly regardless. Lydia isn't ever going to take her place, but she would be filling a need between two consenting adults."

Dave, with the light bulb that just switched on look on his face, said, "Is that why she was so emotional last night? She told me it was because she flunked some type of lab work. I dropped a plate on the kitchen floor, and Lydia immediately flew out of her room. She bent down, and we both grabbed for the same piece, and her hand was trembling. She looked like she'd been crying hard for a while. Was that because of me?"

Steve, now sitting across from Dave, said, "You can't let on that I talked to you. She's told me all of this in confidence, but I believe this is for your well-being as it is for hers. She told me that she's loved you almost from the first day she started to work for you, and your kids, she loves them unconditionally."

Dave, somewhat confused, asked, "So why doesn't she just come out and say that?"

"She told me that she would never show you her emotions until she was sure that you felt the same way, but for your information she told me that she didn't know how much longer she could go on stuffing her emotions. If something didn't happen soon, she would be forced to leave, and she doesn't want to leave because of your kids. Now the ball's in your court, so to speak. What are you going to do with this information?"

Dave put his head in his hands and made a loud sighing sound, then looked up from his hands and said, "I do care about Lydia, but it seems that her feelings for me are much stronger than mine are for her."

Steve replied with some hope, "Don't you want the opportunity to see if your feelings could turn into something other than caring?"

Dave, with a somewhat puzzled look asked, "Why are you trying so hard to make this thing with Lydia work? I know you all too well. Come on, give it up."

Steve gave Dave the crooked wicked smile that he hadn't seen in a long time and Steve said, "I'm hurt deeply by your vague accusations that I'm up to something other than I can't keep a secret and, if you tell Lydia that I gave her up, I'll be totally crushed. I just want to see you happy again. I know that Kelly would have liked Lydia, and in fact Lydia is similar to Kelly in how she deals with her emotions."

Dave smiled and quickly remembered Kelly when Dave and she first met. Then Dave said to Steve, "Okay, I'll give it a try, but I don't want the kids to know, not until I'm sure that this is going to work out. Understand?"

Steve, again with the cheesy smile, said, "You remember when you and Kelly first found out about each other. As I remember I was instrumental in that relationship and look how well that turned out. You guys married and had a family. You can have that again with Lydia."

Dave got serious for a moment and said, "If you think for a minute that Lydia can replace Kelly, then you're sadly mistaken!"

Steve quickly back-peddling said, "No, not ever, Dave. There'll always be just one Kelly. Nobody is trying to replace her. Again, all I want is for you to be happy, and I think Lydia could do that. Just try and give her a chance."

"Okay, but I'm not promising anything."

Steve agreed. Dave could hear Steve's pager going off in his pocket. Steve grabbed it and read the pager, then stopped the buzzer. He got up and said, "Duty calls. Thanks for hearing me out and considering pursuing Lydia."

"Okay, now get out of here and do your real job. Playing cupid isn't going to pay your bills."

Steve, as he left Dave's office with that wicked crooked smile, said, "Yeah, but it's really fun!"

All the way down to the ER Steve kept that silly smile on his face. Once in the ER he stopped at the nurse's desk and Connie, his head nurse, waiting with a chart, looked at him and asked, "What's your reason for your good mood?"

Steve, still smiling, said, "I'll tell you later. Now, what do we have going on?"

She handed him the patient's history form, and Steve looked quickly at it, then said, "Okay, care to join me?"

Connie, with a smile of her own, replied, "I'd love to, Dr. Pratt. Lead on."

Once they got to the exam room and entered the room, both Steve and Connie were all business. Steve, with the file in his hands re-reading parts of the history, said, "Good morning, Mr. Nickerson, I'm Dr. Pratt. It says that you're having some low leg pain along with some coldness and numbness."

"Yes, I've been doing some house renovations, and the leg finally got too painful to continue."

Steve concerned asked, "Can I look at the area that's giving you problems?"

Mr. Nickerson lifted his pant leg up to his knee and painfully rotated his leg inward; Steve was shocked by what he saw. He closely examined a large wound just above his ankle that was jagged that went all the way past his shine bone. The cut was deep and severely infected. In fact, the leg was swollen and looked to have the beginnings of gangrene. Steve asked Mr. Nickerson, "How long have you had this wound?"

"I'm not sure. I'm always cutting myself on one thing or another I'm just not sure how long, is it serious?"

Steve looked seriously at Mr. Nickerson and said, "Mr. Nickerson, I'm not going to sugar coat this, but this may be as serious as losing your leg or even your life."

Mr. Nickerson, in disbelief, responded, "All that drama from a cut on my leg."

At that Steve got upset and replied, "Mr. Nickerson, your neglect of this wound has caused it to get severely infected to the point where your flesh around the wound has begun to be eaten away, and that's gangrene, which could kill you. My nurse is going to start IV antibiotics. I'm going to give you something for the pain, then start to clean out the wound and tissue surrounding the wound. I hope for your sake that when I'm finished, you will still have a leg."

Mr. Nickerson had a startled look on his face and said in a quiet voice, "Please, Dr. Pratt, save my leg!"

Steve laid him down on the exam table and administered the pain medication. He patted Mr. Nickerson on the arm and said, "Don't worry, Mr. Nickerson, I'll do my best to save your leg."

The pain medication was starting to work, and Steve went to work cleaning out the wound. Connie helped irrigate the wound, and after forty-five minutes and cutting away the dead tissue and even some muscle was able to get all the dead tissue. Mr. Nickerson got to keep his leg thus far. The wound size was now almost a half inch deep and was now the size of a softball. Steve packed it and bandaged it heavily. Steve called admitting and got him a bed. He checked his IV and flow rate and increased his antibiotics. A couple of orderlies came and moved him to the second floor. Connie said to Steve, "That man has no idea how close he came to losing his lower leg."

"There's a chance that he still might, so don't go throwing ill wishes on Mr. Nickerson. He can't help it that he was a jerk."

Connie snickered and started to clean up the room.

Meanwhile, Dave was in with a patient and doing a post-operative follow-up exam. The patient was recovering and asking about going home. The patient was a sixty-eight year old female who lived alone. Dave knew that the best solution was that she goes into a nursing home, but he knew from prior experience with this patient that going into a nursing home would surely kill her, so he thought for a moment and asked, "Mrs. Anderson, I want to ask you a forward question, okay?"

"Sure, Dr. Bradfield," said Mrs. Anderson.

"Can you afford home health care? Because I have a skilled nurse who's looking for some extra hours, she'd be a perfect fit for you."

Mrs. Anderson smiled at Dave and said, "I thought you were going to ask me out."

Dave smiled and Mrs. Anderson continued, "Yes, doctor, for a while anyway. My husband left me with good insurance, so maybe between the money and the insurance I can afford it. Does this mean I get to go home?"

"Easy now, Mrs. Anderson, you're moving way to fast. You have at least a week if not more in our fine establishment, then you'll need a rehabilitation hospital, then home."

"I guess I get to look at your pretty face for a while longer, which isn't too bad."

Dave blushed, smiled, and said, "I guess that's a compliment, so thank you, Mrs. Anderson. All we want you to do is continue to get better."

Dave left her room and chuckled to himself. He made a few notes in her chart and went back to his office where the mound of paperwork was still overwhelming. He sat in front of the massive piles of files. Dave took a deep breath and started to weed through the stacks. During that time he got to thinking about Lydia. He knew his kids loved her, especially Sam. She was younger than he, but only by a few years, and right now that wasn't a big concern. He wasn't sure how he felt about Lydia, but thanks to Steve, he knew that Lydia had feelings for him.

Sometimes he wished Steve would just keep these things to himself. He didn't need this right now, but he could hear Steve's voice saying somewhere in his head, there's no better time than the present. Dave shook his head and got back to the mounds of paperwork in front of him. He chose to work through lunch to see if he could make some type of dent in the stacks. Rose came in around six that evening and said, "Dr. Bradfield, why don't you call it good, for today. Tomorrow is another day. You've made some headway."

Dave looked up and said to her, "That seems like sound advice. Good night, Rose."

Rose left his office, went back to her desk, got her things, and left. Dave did the same. He stopped by the ER on his way out just to check with Steve on any last minute pointers, but luckily for Dave he was busy with a patient. He left the hospital and drove home. All the way home he was thinking about what Steve had told him. Dave wasn't sure what or how he was going to handle this situation.

When he arrived home, dinner was ready as usual. Dinner was great as always, and tonight Dave let Lydia know how much he appreciated her and what she meant to his family. Lydia wasn't used to Dave going to such lengths to praise her, and she thought something wasn't right. So she quickly focused on the children and said, "Sam, its' bath time. J.J., if I'm not mistaken, you still have math and some science to finish. Now you both get going. Sam, I'll be up in a minute to start your bath."

Dave said as soon as the children were out of ear shy, "You've been in this house long enough to call me by my first name."

"Dr. B, it's a sign of respect that I don't use your first name."

"Lydia, you're an adult and I'm an adult. Two adult friends can call each other by their first names and have no disrespect to either adult."

Lydia thought about that for a moment, then said, "If you insist, but do you mind if I call you David instead of Dave? Dave just sounds so informal."

"Sure, if you feel okay about that. Why don't you go study and I'll give Sam her bath."

"Dr. B, I mean, David, I can give her her bath. My studies will wait a little while longer."

Dave touched her shoulder gently and said, "I insist."

Dave got up and went upstairs. Lydia knew something was up. She finished cleaning the kitchen, went into her room, and called Steve. Steve, who was still at the hospital and was with a patient when she called, the call went to voice mail and Lydia, left a message. She told Steve to call her back as soon as he was available.

After Dave was done with Sam's bath and put her to bed, he came back down stairs to check on J.J. He went into the study and asked, "How much more do you have left, son? It is starting to get late."

J.J., closing his math book, he yawned and said, "I just finished up, dad."

He put his book back in his book bag and brought it out by the front door. J.J. kissed his dad and said, "Good night, dad, and stop trying so hard with Lydia. Just let it happen."

Then he quietly went up the stairs to his room.

Dave looked at him as he walked up the stairs and thought that he was becoming a great young man, and a perceptive one at that. The house was quiet, and he went by Lydia's door. There was still a light on, but he wasn't sure what to do, so he did nothing. He went back into the den, turned the television on, and channel surfed for a while. Lydia was studying, but also waiting for Steve to call her back. Finally, almost an hour later Lydia's phone vibrated, and she picked it up quickly. Lydia quickly asked, "Did you spill my secret to Dr. B?"

Steve, acting innocent, asked, "No, what makes you think that?"

"Well, for starters, he wanted me to call him by his first name. Then if that wasn't weird enough, he complimented my cooking and how I was such an asset to his family. All of which were out of the ordinary for Dr. B, so I figure that you let him in on our secret."

Steve cringed on the other end, but acted hurt and defeated, and said, "I'm not sure what's going on with Dave, but I hadn't seen him all day. The ER was a mad house and in fact still is. So I'm sorry if you think I told, but I promise you that I didn't."

Lydia, sounding apologetic, replied, "Okay, I'm sorry for blaming you, but you're the only one I've told my secret to and, when Dr. B came home and started to act that way, I just jumped to the conclusion that you told. I'm sorry for doubting you."

They both hung up their phones, and Steve breathed a sigh of relief and quickly called Dave on his cell phone as not to draw attention by dialing the home number. Dave picked the phone up and saw that it was Steve and answered it immediately. Steve asked, miffed, "Are you trying to blow things with Lydia even before things get started?"

"I thought I was doing what you told me to do."

"Well, stop it, because I just got off the phone with Lydia, and she thinks I ratted her out to you, which I lied and told her that I didn't. I told her that I hadn't seen you all day. You need to stop trying so hard. Just let things develop on their own. It's much better that way."

After about a month of letting things run its own course, Lydia was frustrated and Dave was just uncomfortable. One night when both kids were at sleep-overs, Lydia and Dave were alone and in the same room. They both started to speak at the same time. Then they stopped abruptly, then Dave said, "Lydia, you know that I couldn't have survived this last year without you. You've been invaluable to me and my kids. In fact, with you, my children have flourished. I know that there's nobody who can replace Kelly, but I also know that Kelly would want me to find the right woman and even maybe someday get married again. I know Kelly would have liked you. You and she would have been fast friends."

Lydia sat there stunned and at the same time mesmerized by his words. Dave continued, "What I'm tripping all over my tongue trying to say is that I have feelings for you, and I'd like to see where those feelings will take us. That is, if you feel the same?"

Lydia's eyes about popped out of her head. She had to gather herself before she could ever speak, then she managed to say, "I've wished and hoped and even prayed for those words to come out of your mouth. You must know by now that my feelings for you are true and real."

"Yes, Steve told me how you felt and that you had hid your emotions, and they were starting to get the best of you. But with all this talk about feelings, I must make one rule and that is the kids mustn't know until we're sure where this relationship is going. Agree?"

"I totally understand and think that's for the best."

Dave got up from the table and so did Lydia. They both started to clear the dishes when Dave reached for the same dish as Lydia. First their hands met, then they looked at each other and moved closer together. Dave moved in even closer, and Lydia put her arms around him, Dave kissed her slowly at first, then before either of them realized, their passion was controlling every movement. Then Lydia gasped and pulled away. Dave looked at her, and she quickly doubled over and went to the floor in a heap. Dave, right by her side, asked, "What's wrong?"

Lydia said through gasps of pain, "My stomach hurts badly, been drinking antacids."

"You most likely have an ulcer. Do you think you can make it to my car with my help, so we can get you to Bay County?"

Lydia replied, still in pain, "Yeah."

When Dave helped her up, she moaned in pain and, with his assistance, she made it to the car.

Dave drove to the ER right into the ambulance bay. A nurse came out, and before she saw that it was Dr. Bradfield, she was yelling at him that he couldn't park in the ambulance bay. Dave got out of the car, then the nurse realized who she was yelling at and stopped immediately. Dave yelled at the nurse to get a gurney, and she did as she was told.

Dave and the nurse got Lydia onto the gurney and rolled her inside. Dave said to the nurse, "Go get a gurney and then go get Dr. Pratt!"

The nurse brought Dr. Pratt to treatment room three where Dave was taking Lydia's vital signs and getting ready to start an IV. Steve entered the room and asked, "What's wrong, Dave?"

Dave looked up at Steve and said, "Most likely its ulcers. As much pain as she's in, one might have burst."

Steve grabbed the hand-held sonogram machine, put some lubricant on the wand, and rubbed it over the area where Lydia's pain was. Sure enough, he saw a couple of spots and looked like one had indeed burst. Steve put away the wand and said to Lydia, "Lydia, one of your ulcers has burst, and we need to operate now. Are you allergic to any medications?"

Lydia, barely conscious, shook her head side to side. Then she passed out. Dave finished with the IV and Steve said to Dave, "Why don't you wait for me in the surgical waiting room."

"I thought I could lend you a hand?"

"No. Titus is going to help me. You have an emotional connection, and you're too close to this. Titus and I can handle it. It looks to be pretty straightforward."

Dave objected, but knew that Steve was right. Steve and Titus rushed Lydia into the operating room, and Dave paced the entire time she was in surgery. Finally, about two hours later, Steve came out and Dave met him in the middle of the waiting room and asked, "Well?"

"The ulcers were large, and we removed all of them. The one that had ruptured had gone through the stomach wall, so we repaired that as well. She's going to be off of her feet for at least a couple of weeks, but she should make a full recovery. She'll be transferred to a regular room in about an hour."

Then Dave looked down at his feet, then back to Steve and said, "I caused all this. She kept her emotions all bottled up. Why didn't I see the signs earlier and all of this could've been avoided?"

Steve put a hand on Dave's shoulder and said, "You can't blame yourself. I'm just glad you were with her when she had this last attack. If she was by herself, she could have died. I'll let you know what room she'll be transferred to just as soon as I know."

Dave went back to his office and sulked until Steve called and told him that she was in room 321. Steve said to him, "Why don't you go home. She'll sleep through the night, and you should go home and get some sleep as well."

Dave humored him by saying that he might. Steve knew that his request would fall on deaf ears and that he wouldn't go home, but since Steve was on call that night, he went in and checked on Lydia and, sure enough, Dave was camped out in her room. Steve was somewhat aggravated at Dave and said, "Are you staying out of obligation because you think this is your fault or do you really care about her that much?"

Dave looked at Lydia, who was sleeping, then back at Steve and said, "To be honest with you, I believe it's both."

Steve put both hands up in the air in a surrender-type of position and said, "Whatever floats your boat!" and he left Lydia's room.

The next morning Lydia came to and Dave was right by her bedside. He said to her, "Good morning."

"Am I okay," asked Lydia?

"Yes, you're going to be fine. You had some pretty nasty ulcers, but Steve and Dr. Titus fixed you right up."

"Why didn't you do the surgery?"

Dave looked down at the floor, then back at Lydia and said, "Steve thought it would be better if he and Titus did the surgery because of my emotional involvement."

Lydia was somewhat surprised by that, but didn't reply to what Dave had told her. She slowly closed her eyes and continued to sleep on and off for the rest of the day. That afternoon Steve came in and Dave wasn't in the room. Lydia opened her eyes and looked at Steve with tears in her eyes. "Are you okay? Are you in pain?"

Lydia replied with tears streaming down her face. She took a deep breath and gathered herself and said to him, "Steve, this isn't going to work. I'm planning to drop out of school, and I'm going to go back home to recuperate. I'll help Dr. B find his replacement, but then I'm leaving. It breaks my heart to leave him and his children, but for both our sakes I can't be here any longer. Physically and emotionally, I'm not strong enough to wait until Dr. B is ready to have the same kind of feelings I have for him. I know that he said that he does, but he still loves his dead wife, and I'm not about to push him into something that he's not ready for. Now I just have to find the strength to tell him."

Steve was caught off guard by this decision. Then Steve finally said, "Obviously you've thought about this for a while."

"Yes, I was trying to tell him when I had my ulcer attack. Do you have any words of wisdom for me?"

"I think you just have to come right out and tell him. He'll be upset, if not for himself, but for his kids. I know they love you."

Lydia, crying now, replied through her crying, "I know that's the hardest part I love them as if they were my own kids."

Steve patted her on her shoulder and tried to comfort her when Dave walked in. He got all alarmed and asked, "Are you okay, Lydia? What's wrong, Steve?"

"Medically, there's nothing wrong; Lydia is just emotional right now. I'll leave you two alone," replied Steve.

Dave went to her bedside, sat next to her, held her hand, and asked, "What's wrong, Lydia?"

Lydia tried to compose herself, took a deep breath in and let it out slowly, then said, "Dr. B, I'm going home to recuperate. I'm dropping out of school, but don't worry, I'll help you find another nanny and housekeeper."

Dave couldn't understand where this was coming from, and he said confused, "We don't want another nanny; we have you. Take all the time you need to recover, but please don't leave. Don't think of me, but think about my kids. They both have grown emotionally attached to you. It would crush them if you left."

Lydia started to cry again and said through her crying, "Believe you me, if there was any other way, I'd do it, but I'm not strong enough emotionally to stay and know that the feelings are only one-sided. I love your children as if they were my own, but if I don't go I'm afraid I may lose myself emotionally, then I'll be no good to anybody. Please understand. I already have a couple of people in mind as my replacements. I'll set appointments up as soon as I'm able."

Dave pleaded with her, "Please, Lydia, I'll show you more love and affection. If you don't want to be a live-in anymore, I can get you an apartment close by the house. Please, Lydia, think of J.J. and Sam."

Lydia, now crying harder, replied, "I am thinking about the kids I just-"

Then she got a strange expression on her face and started gasping for breath. Dave quickly reacted and put her on some oxygen. That didn't help. He pressed the nurse call button and yelled, "Need some help in here stat!"

Steve was at the nurse's station, and he and another nurse came running into the room. Dave yelled at Steve, "Help her. She can't breathe!"

Steve quickly got the equipment and intubated her, and the nurse bagged her. Then the nurse hooked Lydia to the vent. Steve pushed a couple of drugs into her IV and still no relief. Dave watched in horror as Lydia quickly faded. Then her breathing started to slow and she started to stabilize. Dave and Steve both breathed a sigh of relief.

For the next several hours it was touch and go for Lydia. She had developed a pulmonary embolism that affected her lungs. The medication that Steve gave her slowly was starting to help. She spent the next forty-eight hours in the intensive care unit as a precaution, with Dave at her bedside through it all.

During the second day Lydia finally started showing signs of regaining consciousness. Dave was relieved. Once she was fully conscious she smiled at Dave, and Dave said to her, "You had a pulmonary embolism that affected your lungs. Steve gave you medication that's helping."

Lydia pointed to the tube in her mouth. Dave said, "We'll take it out in the next day or so. Right now we want the machine to breathe for you so that your lungs can heal from the embolism. So be patient and rest."

Lydia nodded that she understood. Dave held her hand and said softy to her, "I owe you an apology. I know you love my kids. It was unfair to throw them up to you like that. We'll all get along without you, although it'll be hard. We have grown, thanks to you, and all the support and love that you've given me and my family. When you're ready and, if you want to, the door to our home will always be open for you."

Dave, with tears in his eyes, bent down and kissed Lydia softly on the cheek. Lydia also had tears and motioned for something to write on. Dave handed her a pad of paper and a pen. She wrote on the pad, "Thank you for understanding."

She showed it to Dave, and Dave nodded, but didn't verbally reply, but he did say, "You rest now, and I'll check on you later."

Lydia was in the intensive care unit for one more day, and Steve ended up taking the breathing tube out that same day. As soon as she could breathe regularly and her oxygen saturation level was above 80%, Steve moved her to a regular room.

She remained in the hospital for two more days, and that was where she said her tearful goodbyes to Sam and J.J. The children understood that she needed to go home and rest and recover, but it didn't make the news any less hard to accept. Dave reassured his kids that Lydia wasn't going to be gone forever, that she would come and visit when she could. That helped somewhat. After the kids left, Lydia said to Dave, "I told you that I'd help you find another nanny, and I have a friend whom I think would be perfect. I'll call her and set up an interview. Is tomorrow okay with you?"

Dave said with tears welling in his eyes, "That would be fine, Lydia. I want to thank you again for everything you've done for this family. We will never forget you." Both Dave and Lydia hugged.

The next day, Lydia was released from the hospital and got packed. Both she and Dave were waiting for Lydia's friend to come and interview for her job. She arrived, and Lydia introduced her to Dave. Her name was April Moore, and she was a lot like Lydia. She was a student, but a little older than Lydia was, and she was newly married. Dave and both of the kids seemed to like her, and that was a load off Lydia's mind.

The next morning before anybody in the Bradfield house was awake; Lydia loaded up her car and took one last look at the house. With tears rolling down her cheek she got into her car and drove away slowly. When Dave got up and realized that she was gone, he felt that all too familiar pang of loss, then the morning hustle and bustle started with the kids, and April was knocking at the front door.

J.J. answered the door and invited her in. She jumped right in and started to make breakfast. Once lunches were made, and both kids were out the door and had caught their bus. April and Dave sat down and went over times and duties, and of course, her salary. Once that was done, April finished up and she also gave Dave her schedule at school, which included mostly night classes, but on Wednesday she had a ten o'clock class in the morning that she could get to, then come back and be there when the kids came home from school. Dave thought it sounded like everything would work out, but missed Lydia already.

Now that she was gone, he missed her, and that hurt something awful. But, as usual, Dave bit down hard on his lower lip, swallowed hard, and shoved his emotions to the back burner and went to work. Steve saw him as he came into the hospital and asked, "How are you doing?"

"I'm not going to lie to you. This hurts, and what hurts even worse is that I have nobody to blame but myself. If I was more like you, I wouldn't be in this position."

A nurse came up to Steve and handed him a chart. He glanced at it, and Dave started to walk away. Steve shouted after him, "Come find me around lunch, okay?"

Dave waved after him, but didn't answer. Dave went toward the elevators, and Steve went back into the emergency room, looked at the chart in his hand, and called out the name on the chart.

CHAPTER 4

When Sarah first entered the emergency room at Bay County, it wasn't busy. The triage nurse who first saw her took her history. She told the nurse that she was helping her husband move a large dresser into their new house and into a bedroom when her arm got pinned between the door jamb and the dresser and, when her husband tried to move it off her arm, Sarah felt her arm break. The triage nurse asked her more routine questions, and then let her go back out into the waiting room.

The nurse saw Steve had handed the chart to him, and he went back out into the ER and called her name. Sarah got up from the chair and, supporting her right arm, followed Steve into a treatment room. Steve quickly looked at the chart, then at Sarah. "So you think you broke your arm moving a dresser."

He examined the arm and there was a definite deformity in both bones just below the elbow.

"I'll call for a portable x-ray. They should be up in a few minutes, and it looks like from what information you gave to the triage nurse that, other than moving heavy dressers, you're in good health. Do you need something for the pain? Your blood pressure is slightly elevated," said Steve.

"It does hurt, but I need to drive myself back home, so can you make it something light," asked Sarah?

Steve thought that it was sort of odd that her husband didn't even bother to come with her, but then Sarah added, "My husband and I just bit off more than we can chew by trying to move by ourselves, but they wanted so much money that we thought we could do it ourselves. I was hoping that it wasn't broken."

The radiology technician came in with the portable x-ray machine, and Steve stepped outside for a minute while he shot the x-rays. When Steve came back into the treatment room, the technician was finished and the x-rays were on the light board. The technician left, and Steve went over and studied the x-rays. Then he went back and sat next to Sarah, who was sitting on the exam table. Steve said to her, "It looks like you're officially done moving furniture; you've broken your arm in two places just below the elbow. You said to me and to the triage nurse that you had no prior medical history, but it looks like you have an old healed fracture, but it doesn't look as if it was medically fixed. When did that occur? Can you tell me about that?"

Sarah didn't say anything for a moment, then she replied, "Before I was married, I used to teach rich business men how to play racquetball and squash at the New York City Athletic Club. I must have hurt it then and never realized that I'd broken it. How long will I be in a cast, doctor?"

"Six to eight weeks," replied Steve.

Steve gave Sarah an injection that was the equivalent of Advil, but with more of a kick. The nurse was getting the casting material ready when she accidently dropped something from the cabinet that clanged as it hit the floor, and Sarah jumped as if somebody had put a firecracker underneath her. Steve couldn't help but notice this. He didn't say anything to Sarah, but he did make a note of it in her chart. As Steve waited for the medication to take effect he made small talk with Sarah. He asked her, "So you moved here from New York?"

"Yes, my husband was in the military, and he just got out and recently got a job working for Zenon in the technical branch. He worked with computers in the military and this is his first job in the civilian world," replied Sarah.

"That is great. Welcome to Bay County. You will like the small town atmosphere that we have here. How long have you and your husband been married," asked Steve?

"Almost four years."

"Do you still teach racket sports?"

"No, we moved around a lot when my husband was in the military, so I'm just a housewife now."

Steve checked Sarah's arm and said, "Okay, Sarah, I believe the medication has worked. I'm going to set your arm, but you still may feel some pressure. Let me know if it's too much and I'll give you some more medication."

Steve and the nurse both gently grabbed her arm, and the nurse pulled, and so did Steve. The bones went back into place, then immediately Steve casted the arm. As he was casting the arm Steve thought it was strange that she didn't flinch as the bones were being put back into place. He finished casting the arm, then gave her a prescription for a mild pain killer and told her that if in six weeks she didn't have a doctor, she could come back and he'd be glad to take the cast off. Sarah was grateful to him and thanked him.

Sarah left, and Steve made a few more notes in her chart and put it back in the large stack at the nurse's desk. As Steve turned around from putting the chart down, a nurse handed him another chart, and Sarah was temporarily forgotten.

The next patient was a sixty-year-old man, and his name was Morris Fagan. He was a repeat patient. Most of the time, he was in the hospital, just to have somebody to visit with since he lost his wife last year. Other times he did have legitimate complaints. Morris liked Steve because he paid attention to him, even when he knew his symptoms weren't real. The last time Morris was in the ER Steve just told him that if he got lonely just to come in and if he had time he would talk to him for as long as he could.

Morris understood, but this time Morris's symptoms were real. Morris came into the ER and the triage nurse recognized him, but knew right away that this visit wasn't just social. Morris barely made it to the triage desk where he clutched his chest and fell to the ground. The triage nurse quickly called a code. Steve rushed to the fallen man and quickly felt for a pulse. There was no pulse, so Steve began CPR, and the code team came quickly after he had begun CPR. They quickly took over life-saving measures. Steve got out of their way, but watched in hope that they could resuscitate Morris. The head of the code team looked up at Steve and shook his head. Steve then called time of death; the code team got him on a gurney, and took him down to the morgue.

Most of the staff in the ER either knew Morris personally or knew of him so the staff took the loss to heart and that included Steve. For once Steve was glad when his shift ended. He called Dave, who was still in his office, and asked if he wanted to have a drink. Dave knew by the tone of his voice that it would be more like having several drinks. Steve had been nothing but professional on and off duty, and this was the first time since the decision that he had even wanted to go out. So Dave thought it would be better if he came, so he told Steve that he would meet him in the staff parking lot and that he would drive. Steve was counting on that and was glad to hear Dave's reply. Dave quickly called April and told her that if it wasn't too much of a burden he would be late tonight. April told him that she understood and would be there when he got home.

Both Steve and Dave met at his car, and Steve looked rattled at best. "Do you want to talk about it?"

"Sure, but I need a drink first," replied Steve.

"Instead of going to some loud, smelly bar, why don't we go to my house? We can sit and you can tell me all about what happened and I have beer and anything else you might want."

"Okay, then is it okay if you drive me to work tomorrow?"

"Sure, that's no problem."

Dave and Steve both got into Dave's car and drove to Dave's house. April was startled that Dave was home so early. She quickly got up and went to the door. As she greeted them both she said, "I thought when you called you were going to be later. Is there anything I can get you? There's some left-over dinner in the refrigerator."

"Sorry about the call. We had a change of plans. There's nothing that we need; thank you, April."

"Then I'll see you tomorrow, Dr. Bradfield. You both have a good night."

April left, and Dave grabbed beer and chips from the kitchen and they both went into the den. They both opened their beers and took long drinks form their bottles. Steve held on to his, and Dave set his down on the coffee table in front of him. Steve took a long deep breath and said, "Did you know Mr. Morris Fagan?"

"Yes, I treated Morris for congestive heart failure last year either right before or right after his wife died. Why?"

Steve once again took a long drink from his beer and said, "He came into the ER today and collapsed in front of the triage nurse. From all indications he was dead before he hit the floor. We assumed a massive heart attack. I did CPR, then the code team did their thing without any success."

"I know that you were fond of Morris, and I'm sorry that he's gone, but there's something else bugging you. What is it?"

Steve finished his beer and quickly opened a second while Dave continued to drink his first. Steve tried to dodge the question. He said instead, "How is the new girl April working out?"

Dave looked cross at Steve and said, "She's just fine. The kids and I are getting use to her."

After Steve took another long drink from his beer he said, "I had a new patient come in today, and I can feel it in my bones that she's being abused by her husband, but I can't prove it."

Dave asked, "What makes you think that?"

"She came in with a broken arm; her arm was broken in two places. The type of break that she had wasn't consistent with the story that she gave me. When I was setting her arm a nurse dropped something behind her, and she jumped like a bomb had gone off. She also had an old fracture that wasn't medically fixed, and what is weird, when she talked about her husband, she never called him by name, always referred to him as my husband; so when I add all these situations up I come up with abuse," said Steve.

Dave took a drink, finished his first beer, and said, "I know that things may seem suspicious, but until you have more proof and or legitimate documentation, then all you're doing is assuming, and you know as well as anybody that you can't assume anything."

"You know me all too well, Dave. Have you heard from Lydia since she left?"

Dave shook his head no and asked, "Do you want to stay the night?"

Steve said, "Yes, if you don't mind."

"That's fine, do you work tomorrow?"

"Yes and no. I have to go to Cameron tomorrow to work at the women's shelter. I need to be there by nine, and since it's almost a forty-five minute drive, if you can just drop me off by my car in the morning that would be great," replied Steve.

"Okay, that won't be a problem. Do you want to sleep on the pull-out in here or on the couch in the living room?"

"Here is fine."

Dave got up and started clearing bottles and Steve said, "So you're not going to talk about your feelings now that Lydia is gone?"

Dave glared at Steve and said as he left the room, "I don't know what you want me to say, I screwed up big time when it came to handling my emotions and Lydia's emotions. I just want her to recover, then maybe sometime in the future I'll give her a call and check on her. Maybe if I'm lucky, which is usually never she may want to come back, but right now I'm not holding my breath. Good night, Steve, I'll see you in the morning."

Dave left the den, and Steve made himself comfortable.

The next day Steve worked a long day at Cameron, and by the time he got back to Bay County it was almost midnight. Steve got home and settled down quickly. He was sound asleep by ten after twelve. His morning alarm jolted him awake, and he rolled over and almost fell back asleep, but instead forced himself up and out of bed and into the shower. Once out of the house he felt somewhat better. He grabbed a yogurt, got dressed, and headed out of the house.

The morning started out slow, which he was thankful for, but by mid-morning the pace picked up quite a bit. Then by late afternoon it slowed down again. During that time Steve was trying to get caught up on paperwork when he was paged to the ER from his office. One of the nurses greeted him with a patient's chart and said to Steve, "The patient said that she only wanted to see you, Dr. Pratt."

The nurse rolled her eyes and handed Steve the chart. Steve looked at the chart and saw that Sarah was back in the ER. He quickly looked at the triage nurse's notes, then he entered the treatment room. A female nurse followed Steve into the treatment room, which was hospital policy. Steve said, "Sarah, back again."

Sarah looked up and, when she did, Steve almost gasped, but maintained his composure. The whole right side of her face looked like she'd been punched repeatedly. On closer examination there were even cuts on her skin. Her right eye was almost swelled shut. Steve was shocked that a man could do this to supposedly somebody he loved. Steve told the nurse to get him some ice packs and also he wanted a cut-down tray. Steve said sternly to Sarah, "Okay, Sarah, what happened?"

Sarah cleared her throat and said, "My husband and I were painting and the paint can fell off the ladder. My hands were full and, as I looked up, the paint can hit me in the face."

Steve got up close to Sarah's face and could see knuckle impressions on her cheek. He felt along her cheek bone to make sure that the bone wasn't broken, and it wasn't. Steve said, "Look, Sarah, you don't have to cover for your husband. I can see where his knuckles left marks in your cheek."

Sarah's expression changed, and she became agitated quickly. She said with her voiced raised somewhat, "Look, Dr. Pratt, I'm very accident prone. I've told you that already. I told you what happened!"

Before Steve could argue with her further, the nurse came back in with the ice packs and a cut-down tray. Steve, instead of continuing the argument, said, "I'm going to have to make a small incision on your eye lid so the swelling and fluid build-up won't continue to put pressure on your eye and cause you any permanent sight damage."

Steve placed the ice packs on her face and directed her to lie down on the treatment table.

He quickly lanced her eye lid, and a large amount of blood discharged from the wound. The wound itself only required a couple of sterile-strips. There was no need for stitches. Steve put a sterile dressing over the eye and gave Sarah instructions. "Okay, Sarah, you need to leave this dressing on for the first twenty-four hours. If after you remove it you have any blurred vision or bad headaches, you need to come back in and see me," said Steve.

Sarah understood and Steve asked, "How is your arm? Is your cast still fitting okay?"

"My arm is good. It doesn't hurt anymore," replied Sarah.

Steve had to try one more time and he said, "Look, Sarah, there's no reason that you have to stay with a man who beats you. I know several shelters for battered and abused women that I can have here within a few minutes."

Sarah interrupted Steve, quickly sat up, and said again with her voiced raised, "For the last time, nobody has hit me, ever! Am I done here?"

Steve nodded, and Sarah got up and stormed out of the treatment room and out of the ER. Steve slammed his fist on the exam table, turned toward the nurse, and said, "Man, Shelly, I blew it. I know her husband is beating on her, but if she doesn't come clean about it, there's nothing I can do."

"Have you checked other hospitals to see if somebody matching her description was ever treated for domestic violence before," asked Shelly?

"Shelly, you're a lifesaver, literally."

Steve went into his office and did exactly what Shelly told him to do, but unfortunately there weren't any matching patients at area hospitals, then he remembered that Sarah had told him that they moved around a lot because her husband was in the military, so he decided to check military bases around the Bay County area. Steve sent out the search, then got called away. An ambulance was bringing in a potential drowning victim. Once the ambulance arrived, the EMT's open the back doors to the ambulance and Steve could smell alcohol on the patient. Steve looked at the EMT and asked, "What is this? I thought you said a potential drowning?"

As the EMT's rolled out the gurney with the patient, Steve could see that his clothes were wet, but the patient had no signs of having been under the water. The EMT said, "That's the call that we answered a possible drowning. We found the man face-down in a plastic kiddy pool. I gave him one rescue breath and he coughed up a little water. He told me thanks in slurred speech, closed his eyes, and went to sleep. Several times I had to check for a pulse to see if he was still alive because he'd been so quiet. Besides reeking from booze, all of his vitals are normal. I even took a blood glucose test and it was normal as well. I figure you could give him a banana bag and send him on his way."

"Take him to treatment room two," replied Steve.

The EMT pushed the gurney inside the emergency room and into treatment room two. They transferred the man from the gurney to the hospital treatment room exam table and the EMT took his gurney and left the room. Steve looked at the man and understood what the EMT meant. He was so quiet that he didn't even look like he was breathing. Steve checked his vitals. All were normal. He checked another blood sugar test and again it was normal. Steve took a blood test so he could see how high his alcohol level was going to be. When Steve drew the blood, the man moaned and mumbled something, but then went right back to sleep. Steve shook his head and said to the nurse in the room, "I bet you that his blood alcohol level is at least five times over the limit."

"My guess it's more like six or seven times," commented the nurse.

Steve sent the blood work to the lab and started the patient on a banana bag, which is just dextrose, electrolytes and other fluids that are lost when alcohol is involved. Steve said to the nurse, "When his blood work comes back, come find me or if he wakes up, I'll be in my office."

The nurse understood. In the ER it was an extremely slow evening. Steve was anxious to see if he got any responses to the e-mail that he'd sent out to the area military bases. Once in his office he quickly went to his computer and pulled up his e-mail. There was a response from a Doctor Jean McNeese. Steve opened the e-mail and read it to himself quickly. At the end of the e-mail Dr. McNeese left a phone number. The e-mail said that she treated a female patient about three months ago fitting the description that Steve had given her. The e-mail said that she was seen four times in a period of a month, and her injuries were inconsistent with the stories she gave. Steve wanted more information and started to call Dr. McNeese when the nurse busted into his office and said, "Dr. Pratt, the blood work is back on or drunk in treatment room two and he's beginning to wake up."

The nurse handed him the lab report, and the man's alcohol level was six times over the legal limit. Steve was somewhat impressed that one man could drink that much and still be alive. He went into treatment room two, and the man was sitting up wide awake, stretching and yawning as if he'd just woken from a long night's sleep. "Can you tell me your name?"

The man finished yawning and said, "My name is Joseph Lang, and I want to thank you, doctor, for helping me tonight."

"Do you know what happened to you this evening," asked Steve?

"Yes, I do, doctor, and I'm sorry for any inconvenience."

"You're nonchalant about this whole situation; I take it this isn't the first time something like this has happened?"

Joseph, somewhat embarrassed, replied, "You're right, doctor, and again I'm sorry for the trouble I put you through. Can I go now?"

Steve looked at the banana bag, and it was more than halfway emptied so Steve discontinued the IV and told Joseph Lang that he was ready to go. Joseph hopped down from the exam table, wet clothes and all. He even had a little swing in his step as he walked out of the treatment room and out of the emergency room. Both Steve and the nurse looked at each other and shook their heads at one another. Steve went back to his office because he was anxious to call Dr. McNeese and try to get more information on Sarah.

Steve picked up the phone and dialed the number on the bottom of her e-mail. Dr. McNeese answered the phone and Steve said, "Dr. McNeese, this is Dr. Pratt at Bay County. I wonder if you have a few minutes to talk with me. I believe we have an abuse victim in common."

"Yes, Dr. Pratt, I replied to your e-mail. I believe it's the same woman. The name she gave me was Mary Cook, and the story that she gave me was she was new and her husband had just moved into on-base housing. Her injuries weren't consistent with moving injuries. I documented my feelings about abuse and, when I confronted her about it the third time she showed up in my ER, she got defensive, but she stuck to her story. Another thing I thought was weird is that she never called her husband by his name. It was always my husband this or that. Does any of what I mentioned sound familiar?"

Steve, smiling on the other end of the phone said, "Yes, all of it right down to the moving story, but her name has changed. She's now Sarah something. I can't remember a last name. I don't have her chart in front of me. Did you treat her for a broken wrist, but according to the x-ray it looked like it wasn't surgically set?"

Dr. McNeese, who was actually looking at the chart, said, "Yes, my notes said that she refused surgery, which was needed to fix the wrist properly. All she would allow me to do was to cast it. Just a warning; I saw her four times. The last time she came in by ambulance, and she was almost beaten to death. She had numerous bruises and lacerations, broken bones, and she was unconscious for two days. When she did come to, she freaked that she was actually in the hospital, and the next morning she was gone. She would have had to literally drag herself out of here, and she was in bad shape."

"So did you or the police ever get to see the husband," asked Steve.

"No, I hope you have better luck than I did. I'll fax you her entire file and all my notes. Something may help you break this abusive chain. Thank you for calling, Dr. Pratt, and good luck."

"Thank you, Dr. McNeese, for the information. This shows some light on just how bad this patient needs our help."

Both doctors hung up the phone, and soon Steve's fax machine started and the file was being faxed. Once the whole file had been faxed he put all the pages together, sat back down, and read it. It was just as Dr. McNeese had told him over the phone. One thing that he didn't expect to see was the husband's name. But as Steve thought about it, in the military you've to give the name since Sarah was a dependent of his.

The military doctors wouldn't treat Sarah without his name. Steve wasn't sure if the name was any good, but it was sure worth a try. He called Cindy Winslow, who worked for the Bay County Sheriff's Department. Once upon a time Cindy and Steve were pretty hot and heavy, but their jobs got in the way, and they parted company as friends. Once he got Cindy on the phone, she was glad to hear from Steve and wanted to know what she could do for him. "Cindy, I am sorry, this isn't a personal call, but it may be a life or death situation."

"Go ahead, anything that you need," said Cindy.

"I have a female patient who's in trouble. I have a name I want you to try and find an address or phone number or whatever you can find," said Steve.

"Okay, give me his name, and I'll see what I can do."

"His name is Jake Winter; he's just out of the military."

"I'm running his name now. How have you been," asked Cindy?

"Good. You know me, all work and no play," said Steve.

"I hardly doubt that, but if you say so," replied Cindy.

Steve asked, "How about you? What is going on in your world?"

"I'm doing well. In fact, I'm engaged to be married next year. He's a fellow officer," replied Cindy.

"That is great, Cindy. Congratulations," said Steve.

"I have your information. Your man Jake Winter has a home address of 3218 North Addison Avenue, apartment 2A. He also has a sheet. He has three domestic violence charges against him, two restraining orders. One has expired, and one is about to expire. He spent a few days in lock-up for a drunken and disorderly charge, but the bill was paid and he was released. All of these charges have either been dropped or time has expired. He has no charges pending, so technically we can't do anything to help you out. So you be careful. This one doesn't like to play well with others," said Cindy.

"I understand. All I really wanted was an address anyway. Cindy thanks for your help, congratulations again on your engagement," replied Steve.

Cindy smiled on the other end of the phone as she hung up the receiver. Cindy went ahead and printed the information out because she knew that if Steve was involved and it dealt with a patient, he was like a bulldog, and once he got his teeth into the situation, he wasn't about to let loose until his patient was treated or in this case out of danger. She took the sheets from the printer and put it in her top drawer just in case she would need it later.

Now that Steve had the information, he wasn't sure what to do with it. He sat staring at the address, when he got a page from the ER that an ambulance was two minutes out. The patient was found in her front yard. Steve shoved the piece of paper with the address into his pocket, went to the ambulance bay, and waited for the ambulance to come in.

Once the ambulance arrived, the EMT's pulled the gurney out and started to give Steve all the information. The EMT told Steve that a thirty-something female was found by a neighbor unconscious in her front yard. Steve took one look at the patient and knew it was Sarah, even though she was beaten so badly that she was almost unrecognizable. The EMT, along with Steve, continued to wheel her into the ER. The EMT knew that Steve was distracted and had to ask, "Dr. Pratt, where do you want to go with this patient?"

Steve snapped out of it and told the EMT to take her to trauma room two. The EMT did as Steve told him. As the EMT unloaded Sarah onto the hospital gurney, Steve quickly pulled the address from his pocket and asked, "Did you find her at 3218 North Addison Avenue, apartment 2A?"

"Yeah, but how did you know," asked the EMT?

"Never mind," Steve said as he shoved the piece of paper back into his pocket.

The EMT took his gurney and left the trauma room, then went back to the ambulance. Steve and a couple of nurses started to treat Sarah. One of the nurses cleaned her face so Steve could see what damage was done, and by the looks there was plenty. Visibly it looked like her orbit, cheek, and jaw bones were all fractured, and she was even missing teeth. She had a couple of deep lacerations, one over her left eye and another just under her cheek bone, which actually exposed the bone. Steve called radiology and said that he needed a full head and neck series in trauma two. The technician that answered the phone said to Steve that somebody would be right up.

After the x-rays were taken, all the fractures in her face were confirmed, and her collar bone was also fractured. Steve cut her shirt off, and as Steve exposed Sarah's torso, the nurse in the room gasped. She apologized for doing so, but Steve was also quite shocked at what he saw. She was one big bruise. The bruises were in a form of a fist, and some looked new and other were already turning green and yellow.

Steve also noticed that she even had bruises on her breasts. He had the radiology technician also take x-rays of her ribs and, sure enough, she had multiple breaks on several ribs on both sides of her chest. Steve called Titus and said that he had a patient in trauma two that needed an orthopedic surgeon. The nurse quickly called Steve to Sarah's side she was starting to regain consciousness.

Sarah couldn't talk because of her jaw being broken, so Steve calmed her and said, "Sarah, you have serious injuries to your face and upper torso. You're going to need surgery. Jake has used you for a punching bag for the last time. If he had hit you any harder or just one more time, he could have killed you."

Sarah grabbed Steve's arm and tears streamed from the one eye that wasn't already swollen shut. She shook her head slowly back and forth in a no motion. Steve steadied her head and said, "Don't worry, Sarah, I won't let him hurt you again."

Sarah lost consciousness, and Titus came into the trauma room, looked at the fractures, and said, "It's amazing how much pain one human being can inflict on another."

Steve didn't reply to Titus, but instead stormed out of the trauma room. He reached into his pocket and took out the scrap piece of paper. He stared at it for a long time, then scrunched it back into his pocket.

By the time Sarah was taken to surgery it was morning, and Steve's shift was over. His replacement was already on the clock working. Dr. Harry Wilson was his replacement, and they said hello to each other in passing. Steve went back to his office, grabbed his things, and was going home, but instead he wanted to see for himself what Sarah's husband looked like.

He parked his car down a little ways from the address on the scrap piece of paper and waited for him to come out. Finally a man came out of the duplex, grabbed the paper from the driveway, then unlocked his car, got in, and drove away. From what Steve could see he was maybe six foot, and he looked to be well-built. Steve wanted to approach him and ask him what sort of man beats his wife almost to death and gets up to go to work like nothing ever happened, but he remained cool and waited for the right time to do just that.

Steve drove away from the duplex and back to his house. Steve tried to wind down and get some sleep, knowing that he would be back working again at midnight that night. He tried to lie down, but all he could see was Sarah bloodied and almost unrecognizable. He must have dozed off sometime that afternoon because when he woke up it was dark outside.

He looked at his watch; it was almost ten in the evening. Then his cell phone rang. It was Titus and he said, "Steve, your patient had a visitor this evening, her husband. Luckily there was a nurse who came into her room because he tried to take her out of the hospital. I think the nurse scared him off. Your patient is a basket-case and has been asking for you. I know you're not due in for a couple of hours yet, but can I persuade you to come in and try to calm her down? I put a lot of my best work into her face; I don't want to see that ruined."

Steve rolled his eyes at Titus's vanity, but told him that he'd be in as soon as he could. He also asked for security to be posted at Sarah's room. Titus told him that he'd already done that, and he told Steve that Sarah was in SICU bed three. Steve thanked him and pushed the off button on his cell phone. Steve took a quick shower, put on a fresh pair of scrubs, and went back to the hospital. Steve went right to SICU to bed three. When he entered, Sarah's eyes lighted up. She had a small dry erase board that she was writing on since she couldn't talk due to her broken jaw that was now wired closed. Her face was heavily bandaged so Steve couldn't tell what work had been done, so he grabbed her chart and read through it quickly. From Titus's notes, it looked like Sarah was in for several more surgeries and some rehab with her facial muscles, and even her smile might be an issue.

Steve put the chart down and went to her bedside. Sarah weakly grabbed for his hand, and Steve let her take it as she grabbed onto it and held it tight. "How are you doing," asked Steve?

Sarah wrote down on the board, "Okay."

"How is your pain," asked Steve?

Sarah wrote down on her board, "Four."

"Good, don't let your pain get any higher. Make sure you call the nurse if you're in pain or anything else is bothering you," replied Steve.

Sarah nodded slowly that she understood. Steve asked, "Can you swear out a warrant for your husband, so he won't come back again?"

Sarah closed her eyes for a moment, then opened them and wrote on her board, "Have tried before, he has a good lawyer."

"But he almost killed you, and he came to the hospital and wanted to check you out against medical advice. I'll back you up one hundred percent. I can testify, and so will Dr. Titus, the surgeon who worked on your face. I can have an officer from the Sheriff's Department here in five minutes, and he'll be in jail in ten minutes."

Sarah wrote on her board, "Then he will be out in fifteen minutes."

"If I could give you a guarantee that he wouldn't be this time, would you swear out the warrant," asked Steve?

Sarah squeezed his hand tighter and wrote on her board, "I don't think you can guarantee that, but I trust you, so yes, I will swear out the warrant." She erased what she'd written and wrote, "I am very scared," and she underlined very.

Steve read the board and said, "I understand. I promise you that he'll never hurt you again."

Her eyes shined through the heavy bandages, and Steve quickly called Cindy Winslow at the Sheriff's Office and told her that he had a patient who wanted to swear out a warrant for the arrest of her husband. Cindy on the other of the phone said, "Let me guess; Jake Winter.

"You're good," said Steve.

"What type of warrant," asked Cindy?

"Attempted murder," Steve replied meaning.

"You're not playing around. I'll be over soon with the paper work. Where's your patient located?"

"Cindy, you are the best. My patient is in SICU room three."

Cindy told Steve that she'd be there soon. Steve put his cell phone back into his pocket, patted Sarah's hand, and reassured her that everything was going to be okay. Steve heard a commotion out in the hallway, and he stepped out of Sarah's room. Standing there in front of the security guard was Sarah's husband. It took every fiber in Steve's body not to go after him and tear him from limb to limb. Steve closed the door to Sarah's room behind him and asked Joe, the security guard, "What's the trouble?"

Jake answered before Joe could, and Jake said, "This rent-a-cop won't let me see my wife."

Steve, trying to hold his temper, replied, "This rent-a-cop that you're referring to is one of our security guards, and he's only following my orders. I'm Dr. Pratt; I'm your wife's doctor."

Jake then walked right up to Steve and said, "Then, doc, let me see my wife!"

Steve stepped out to meet him, but didn't raise a hand. Steve, holding back his temper said to him, "No. Sarah doesn't want to see you."

Jake got even closer to Steve and said, "You can't stop me. I have a right to see her!"

Steve held his ground and his temper and replied, "No, sir, I have the right to make sure my patient is protected and what's in the best interest of my patient, and right now that includes you not seeing her."

Jake got close enough so he was almost nose to nose with Steve. "I guarantee that you don't want to get any closer because, unlike Sarah, I'll hit you back," said Steve softly.

Jake's face got red. He was really mad. Just then Cindy came in with two fellow Sheriff's Officers, went to Sarah's room, then quickly came back out. Cindy said to the officer's, "Please cuff that man."

Jake, confused, and visibly upset said, "For what?"

Cindy, putting the warrant almost in Jake's face, said with a smile, "For attempted murder."

Jake laughed and said, "Go ahead. My lawyer will get me out, then you and me, doc, this is definitely not over, not over by a long shot."

The officers cuffed him and led him away. Cindy stayed behind and asked Steve, "I know what his record is, but do you have any proof of any prior bad actions against Sarah?"

"I have a whole file full from the doctor who treated her at the military base, then the treatment that she was given here at Bay County."

"I have a friend at the District Attorney's office; I'll run this by her and see if it's enough to get this quickly through the system, so he isn't able to get out so quickly."

Steve thanked Cindy, and Cindy left, Steve went back into Sarah's room. Steve told her what happened and she wrote on her board, "He will be so angry," and she underlined the word so.

"Not this time, Sarah. I have a friend who is speaking to the D.A.'s office, and she won't let him get out so quickly. Now, you have Joe right outside, and I'm only a phone call away. You rest now, and I'll check on you later."

Sarah nodded, and Steve went back to the ER. Thank goodness it was a slow night because Steve had a hard time concentrating on anything else than Sarah and what he just witnessed from her husband Jake Winter. It was just about the end of Steve's shift when his phone rang. When he picked it up, the voice on the other end said," Pratt, I'm afraid I have bad news," said Cindy.

"I'm afraid to ask, Cindy. What happened," asked Steve?

"Jake Winter bonded out of jail about an hour ago."

"I thought the D. A was going to see to it that he didn't get out."

"She tried, Steve, but his lawyer argued that he had no priors and that he was an upstanding businessman. The judge posted bail at five hundred thousand and he made that bond. I did, however, make a restraining order stick. He cannot come within five hundred feet of Sarah or he'll be in violation of his bail. The hearing is set for two weeks from today. You and Sarah both need to be at that hearing, so hopefully Jake will go to jail. You also need to know something about Sarah. She's always gotten to this point, but never testified against her husband in open court. I'd watch my back, Steve."

"Thanks for the information."

Steve went upstairs and told Joe the security guard that Jake was out of jail, and he also made him aware of the restraining order in place. Joe understood.

Steve stepped into Sarah's room, and she was sleeping as peacefully as possible considering her broken face. Steve stepped back out and said to Joe, "I'm going home and if there is anything that come up, please don't hesitate to call."

Again Joe understood and in a husky deep voice said, "I got this, Dr. Pratt. Go home get some sleep. You look like you could use some."

Steve smiled, walked down the hall to the elevators and back down to the ER where he made sure his replacement was doing okay, which he was, and Steve went home.

The process of healing was slow and tedious and, with all the physical therapy, that made it just that much harder and slower, but finally Steve was just about ready to discharge Sarah from the hospital.

He was heading to her room to give her the good news when he heard her screaming from her regular room. Steve quickly entered her room and asked, "What's wrong?"

The nurse replied with Sarah in hysterics, "She thought she saw her husband outside her window."

The nurse left, and Sarah rushed into Steve's arms trembling. They had become emotionally attached to one another over the last two weeks. Steve wasn't planning on that happening; it was just something that did. Steve peeled her off, looked at her, and said, "Did you really see him?"

Sarah nodded slowly. She still had some bandages on her face, and her arm was in a sling due to the broken clavicle. Her jaw was still wired, but she could talk somewhat through the wiring. Steve said to her with care, "We only have a few more days till the hearing; you'll be with me until then."

Sarah started to cry and said in somewhat of a mumble, "I don't think I can do this, I'm not strong enough!" She continued to cry.

Steve grabbed her gently, pulled her close, and said to her softly, "You're one of the strongest people I know. If you can survive all the beatings you took from that man for years, then this hearing will be a piece of cake, and I'll be right there with you."

Sarah hugged him tightly, and they both left the hospital. Jake watched from his car that was parked across the street. As Steve drove Sarah to his house, Jake followed a safe distance as not to raise any suspicions.

Once home, Steve got Sarah settled and as calmed down as possible under the circumstances. Steve was supposed to be off for the next couple of days so he could be with Sarah and also could attend the hearing. Steve had just given Sarah some medication to help her sleep when his cell phone rang. He answered it quickly so as not to disturb her. Steve said, "Pratt."

The voice on the other end was Dave's, and Steve knew that meant something was wrong at the hospital. Dave said, "Steve, the refinery downtown, part of the oil distribution center, just blew up. Dispatch called and we're about to get some critically wounded workers. Can you come in? I could use another pair of hands. I've already called in John and Titus."

"I just gave Sarah something to help her sleep. I really don't want to leave her by herself. Can you get somebody, anybody, to come over and stay with her till I can return home?"

Steve heard him flipping through some papers on the phone, and then Dave answered, "I have a floater nurse on the third floor this evening. I will get her to come over. She will be there in five minutes."

"How soon are you expecting ambulances," asked Steve?

"The first are now pulling in," replied Dave.

"I'll be there as soon as your floater comes."

Dave ended the conversation and went out to the ambulance bay. The floater nurse knocked on Steve's door about five minutes later, and Steve quickly introduced himself and told her about Sarah. The float nurse understood, and Steve left for the hospital. When Steve arrived, three ambulances had already been there and gone. Two patients were critical, two with severe burns. One patient had internal trauma, and there were more ambulances on the way. Steve found Titus working on one of the burn patients. Steve asked, "Where do you want me?"

Titus thought for a moment, then replied, "Dave is in trauma one with a patient with internal injuries, and John is in exam three working on another patient. There's another ambulance coming in. Why don't you go meet that and treat as many as you can? My patient isn't going to make it; I'll join you as soon as he passes."

Just then Titus's patient flat-lined and Steve heard the ambulance coming, so he ran toward the ambulance bay and waited for the EMT's to pull the gurney out of the back of the truck. The patient whom the EMT's pulled out of the ambulance had severe crush injuries to his legs. He was screaming and rocking the gurney back and forth because he was in so much pain. "Did you give him something for the pain," asked Steve?

"Thus far we've given him twenty ccs of morphine intramuscular," replied the EMT.

"That would knock out the normal patient. Let's get him to treatment room one. All the trauma rooms are filled."

Steve was already thinking about how he was going to treat this patient, since the morphine wasn't working, but he already had too much on board to switch to another pain medication, so he thought he'd use the same drugs that normally were used to intubate a patient. Steve quickly pushed those drugs, and he had to protect the patient's airway, so he intubated him. Quickly the drugs took effect, then he could treat his injuries more efficiently. He cut the pants off the worker and gasped at the horrible sight.

The worker's legs were crushed; the right leg was totally beyond repair and would have to be amputated. The left leg looked somewhat more solid, but his femur was broken in numerous places. So was the tibia and fibula. The foot on the left leg looked unharmed. Steve got x-rays of both legs, even though he knew that the right would have to be amputated.

Titus joined Steve in the treatment room and confirmed Steve's diagnosis. Titus said, "Let me take him up to the operating room and see if I can save his left leg at least. I'd hate to see this accident make him a paraplegic."

Steve agreed and heard another ambulance pulling up to the ambulance bay. Steve asked Titus, "You got this patient? I'm heading out to the ambulance bay."

Titus nodded, and Steve ran out of the treatment room and met the EMT's as they brought in another patient from the oil refinery. This patient had first and second degree burns on his hands, lower torso, and upper legs. Steve stripped the patient's clothes. He started an IV and added some pain medication, and told the orderlies to take the patient to the burn unit. Steve asked the EMT's, "How many more patients are headed our way?"

The EMT said, after he took a large deep breath, "This is the last. When I left the scene with this patient, the firefighters were getting the fire under control and starting to clean up the area around the refinery."

Steve thanked the EMT for the information, found Dave and said to him, "The last patient was sent up to the burn unit, and if it is okay for you I'm going home and I'll send your floater back to the hospital."

Dave said to him, "That is fine. Thanks for your help."

Steve quickly called home. Sarah anxiously picked up the phone and said nervously, "Are you about done?"

Steve, in a calming voice, said, "Calm down. I'm ready to leave. I'll be home in five minutes."

Steve put the phone back into his pocket and looked at his watch; it was almost one in the morning. He was exhausted and anxious to get home.

Sarah thought that it was late, and the float nurse still had to go back to the hospital and finish her shift, so she told her that she could go ahead and leave. The float nurse said to Sarah, "Dr. Pratt told me that I wasn't to leave this house until he was here."

Sarah smiled at the efficiency and thoughtfulness of Steve, but reassured the float nurse that by the time she got her jacket on and made it to her car, Steve would be home. After much prodding, the float nurse left, and Sarah quickly locked the front door behind the float nurse. She then grabbed the throw off the back of the couch, curled up in the recliner, and waited anxiously for Steve to come and unlock the front door. As she lay in the recliner waiting for Steve to arrive, she heard every noise that the house made, and also she heard the wind and the crickets outside the house. She was letting her imagination get the better of her.

Then she heard a large crashing sound toward the back of the house, and that wasn't her imagination. She quickly got up from the recliner and went to investigate the sound. Her heart was in her throat as she crept around the corner. To her horror, she found her husband standing in the hallway with an evil smile on his face. Sarah began to panic and cry. She still had a few bandages on her face, and those became soaked through quickly with tears and sweat. "Ah, Sarah, you mean that you aren't glad to see me? I think you look beautiful. The work they did on your face is remarkable. How is Dr. Pratt treating you? I bet he's tender and loving and caring with you."

All the time he was talking, she started to walk backwards toward the living room and toward the front door. Then she turned and ran toward the living room. She got to the middle of the room and Jake tackled her and climbed on top of her. Sarah continued to fight, but he was much stronger and overpowered her quickly.

Then she just stopped struggling altogether, because she knew what was going to happen next. When she stopped struggling, this excited him, and he began to rape her forcefully. She felt Jake enter her so roughly that she screamed out in pain, and he continued to push himself deeper and deeper inside her until she thought she would rip apart. Tears streamed down her hot, flushed face, but she continued to lie there motionless with her husband on top of her raping her with such force that she knew she was going to die.

Then she heard something that was music to her ears. She heard the sound of Steve's car pulling into the driveway. Then he came up the walk, onto the porch, and unlocked the front door. Jake pulled out of Sarah, zipped his pants, and yanked her to a standing position by her hair. He pulled Sarah directly in front of him and pulled a gun from the back waistband of his pants, cocked it, put it to Sarah's temple, and said, "Don't move or say a word or I'll shoot him as he walks in, then I'll shoot you."

Sarah wasn't afraid for herself any longer, but now was afraid for Steve's life. The last thing she wanted was to put Steve in danger; he'd done nothing but try and help her from the first moment that he saw her. Sarah did as Jake told her.

Steve opened the front door and entered his house, and there directly in front of him was Sarah with her husband behind her with a gun pointed at her head. Steve, seeing this, dropped everything in his hands, and Steve looked at Sarah with her bandages soaked from tears and sweat. He also noticed a thin line of blood running down the inside of her leg; he guessed that the monster had raped her. Steve also noticed the crazed look in his eyes. Steve thought this could be dangerous for all involved. Just as Steve was gathering his thoughts, Sarah's husband spoke, "I don't know why you've wasted your time with Sarah. There's only one man for her, and that man is me."

Steve was careful about his response and said, "I can see that now. I can see how much you mean to her. As far as I'm concerned, she's all yours."

Jake was somewhat taken back by Steve's statement. This wasn't how his rehearsal was supposed to go. "In fact, I really don't even like her; I was just looking after her medically."

Again, Jake looked perplexed, and Steve slowly started to approach them, forcing both of them backwards more toward the middle of the living room. Jake yelled at Steve to stop and Steve did as he was told. "Why don't you put the gun down and you and Sarah can leave peacefully."

Jake hesitated, then lowered the gun somewhat and, before anybody could make another move, Steve rushed Jake, and Sarah tried to get out of the way. Jake's grip on the gun and on Sarah was strong, and all three wrestled around on the living room floor, then the gun went off four or five times. Then there was silence; nothing moved in the house. Steve's neighbors called the police, and they were there within a few minutes of the gunfire.

The police arrived on scene and proceeded with caution. They entered the house, and the lead officer kicked the gun away from the bodies. He bent down and checked each body as he came to it. Sarah's body was first. She had a single gunshot to the center of the forehead. She had no pulse; she was dead. The next body was Jake, Sarah's husband. He had two bullets center in his chest. He had no pulse and he was dead. Then the lead officer came to Steve's body he had a deep graze wound from just above his right eye and it continued just past his ear. He also had a bullet wound in his right lower shoulder. Any lower and he, too, would have been dead. Steve had a pulse, and the lead officer quickly called the coroner and also the ambulance.

The ambulance arrived quickly, and the EMT's worked to get Steve ready to transport to Bay County. When the EMT's called into Bay County, Titus was covering the ER and he listened to the EMT's transmission and thought he heard him say that Dr. Pratt was the shooting victim that they were bringing in. Titus was so flustered that he made the EMT repeat the name of the patient, and they indeed confirmed that the patient was Dr. Pratt.

When the ambulance arrived, Titus thought that Steve didn't look that bad. His vitals were stable, but he wasn't regaining consciousness. Once in a treatment room Titus tried several different things to bring him around. He tried smelling salts, an ammonia cap, and even tried a small dose of epinephrine. Titus waited for the drug to work, but all it did was make his vitals jump, but then they quickly returned to normal. Titus immediately ordered an MRI and a head CT.

The bullet wound in his right lower shoulder was a through and through wound. Titus cleaned the wound and sewed the wound close. He continuously monitored Steve's vitals, and they remained normal. As Titus was waiting for the results from the MRI and the CT scan, he called Dave and also called a neurologist, Dr. Raymond Moth, one of the top doctors in his field.

Both Dave and Dr. Moth were just getting up since it was almost five in the morning. Dave told Titus that he'd be there just as quickly as he could. Dr. Moth, on the other hand, wasn't so hospitable. He told Titus, "This better be good, Dr. Titus."

Titus rolled his eyes at his rudeness and said as nicely as he could manage, "I have a patient, Dr. Steve Pratt, who has received multiple gunshot wounds. The first wound is a large graze wound that starts just above his right eyebrow and ends just past his right ear. His other wound was a through and through in his right lower shoulder that I've already taken care of. My dilemma is that I can't get him to regain consciousness. His vital signs are normal, and I've already given him a MRI and a CT scan. I have not yet gotten the results back from either of the scans. I need your help. You're the best in the business, and I'm sorry about the early hour."

"I want you to start him on a course of steroids just in case there's any swelling going on. I'll be there in about twenty minutes," replied Dr. Moth.

Titus closed his phone, put it back into his pocket, and did as Dr. Moth wanted. By the time Dr. Moth got there, Titus had both scans back and they looked to be normal. Dr. Moth came in, looked at his chart, and also studied both of the scans, then, said to Titus, "I want another MRI and CT scan, and I also want an EEG."

Despite what Titus thought of Dr. Moth, he did as he was told. Both of the scans were done again, and the EEG was done after Dr. Moth had the new scans. The EEG showed a small elevation in the pressure, and now the MRI and CT showed a mass right below where the graze wound started. Titus said, "His scans were clear just an hour earlier."

"It's the hour that made the difference. You can schedule Dr. Pratt for surgery, and I'll remove the subdural hematoma, and he should regain consciousness," said Dr. Moth.

As they took Steve to the operating room, Dave came into the hospital, spotted Titus, and asked, "What's going on, Titus?"

Titus put a hand on Dave's shoulder and replied, "The EMT's brought Steve in with multiple gunshots. One of the bullets caused a subdural hematoma and we're taking him up to the operating room. The other gunshot wound was a through and through to his lower shoulder which I cleaned up and stitched."

"Do you know what the circumstance around the shooting was?"

"There was some type of disturbance at Steve's house. The police found Sarah and her husband dead on Steve's living room floor. The police said that there looked like there was quite a struggle."

"Thanks, Titus, for taking such good care of Steve. Who's doing the surgery," asked Dave?

Titus said, "Dr. Raymond Moth. He's an excellent surgeon, but not a very nice person."

"Nothing but the best as far as you're concerned, Titus, which is great. I'm going to check in with my secretary, then I'll go up and wait for Steve to come out of surgery," replied Dave.

"I'm going to arrange the ER schedule for a few days, then I'll join you in the OR waiting room," said Titus.

Dr. Moth took almost three hours to completely take out all of the hematoma, and he also did some fancy stitching to close the graze wound. When Dr. Moth finally came out of surgery he found Dave, John, and Titus waiting, and he was sort of surprised. All three doctors got up, and Dave stepped forward and asked, "So how did Steve do in surgery?"

"He came through just fine. The next twenty-four hours will be critical, and I'm sending him back to the SICU," said Dr. Moth.

Dave asked another question, and Dr. Moth didn't want to answer, "Is there going to be any lasting effects?"

Dr. Moth looked directly at Dave, glared at him, and replied, "I'm not going to mince any words with you. We're professionals here. The biggest effect with traumatic injuries such as this is going to be his memory, and also his consciousness will be another issue. You know as well as I do that we still don't have many answers when it comes to the brain. Let us just take this one step at a time. Steve is young and in good physical shape, and that's a plus for him."

Dr. Moth went back into the OR, and all three doctors sat back down. Nobody said anything. Once Steve was moved back into the SICU, Dave sat at his bedside. For the next twenty-eight hours Steve did nothing but lie there motionless and unconscious. Then as the twenty-ninth hour approached, Steve started to regain consciousness. Dave got up from his chair and stood at his bedside. Steve was slow to fully regain consciousness. Dr. Moth came in just as he was fully conscious and stood on the opposite side of the bed from Dave and asked Steve, "Dr. Pratt, how are you feeling?"

Steve replied sluggishly, "My head hurts. Why am I in the hospital? What happened?"

Steve felt the heavy bandage on his forehead, and Dr. Moth said calmly to Steve, "I was hoping you could tell me. What's the last thing you can remember?"

Steve again sluggishly replied, "I remember a big fire at the oil refinery, then I remember going home." Steve got a worried look on his face and added, "Did something happen to Sarah?"

Dr. Moth put a hand on Steve's uninjured shoulder and tried to calm him down. Steve became more and more agitated, insisting about knowing what happened. Steve, almost yelling, said, "Please, somebody! Dave, please tell me what happened!"

Dave looked at Dr. Moth, and Dr. Moth nodded Dave said, "Okay. I'll tell you, but you'll have to calm down."

Steve took a deep breath, tried to slow his breathing down, and looked at Dave. Dave only knew what had happened third handed, because he heard it from Titus, who originally got it from the EMT's who brought Steve into the emergency room. Dave took a deep breath and collected himself, and started slowly, "This is what we've pieced together from the police and from the EMT's who brought you in. The police found you, Sarah, and Sarah's husband on your living room floor. There were signs that a large struggle had taken place. Both Sarah and her husband were pronounced dead at the scene. Does any of this bring back any memories?"

Steve welled up with tears and, with a blank look on his face, replied, "No, I don't remember any of that. You mean that Sarah is dead? How did it happen?"

Steve became very emotional, and Dave placed a hand on his arm and patted it lightly. Dave replied again slowly, "The police think there was a scuffle, and Sarah's husband had a gun. During that scuffle, the gun went off. Sarah was found with a single bullet wound to the head, and her husband was shot twice in the chest."

Tears came freely and, through his tears, he asked, "Will I ever remember?"

"You may. Something this traumatic may take a while. If your memory does start to come back, it'll come in bits and pieces, but you may or may not ever get the whole memory back. Don't try to rush this. If it comes back, it'll come back on its own schedule, not yours. You need to rest now," replied Dave.

That next day had gotten away from Dave. He wanted several times to see how Steve was doing but, something always came up keeping him from doing so. Finally he managed to make it to Steve's room, but it was already the end of the day. Dave entered his SICU room and was shocked to see just how bad he looked. The heavy bandage had been removed, and he had heavy bruising around his face. The graze wound had become dark and swollen. His right eye was almost closed from the swelling. The most disturbing thing was that he was heavily sedated. Dave called Titus and asked if he knew why Steve was so heavily sedated. Titus replied, "I'm not sure. Give me a few minutes and I'll be right there."

Dave sat with Steve until Titus came into Steve's SICU room. Dave asked again as Titus entered the room, "Steve looks bad. Why is he so heavily sedated?"

"It wasn't by choice. We did cold packs on his face and eye area, and that wasn't helping with his pain, so I increased his medication, but that was earlier today before lunch. I haven't increased it since then," replied Titus.

Both Dave and Titus opened his chart and quickly read through it. There wasn't any other entry except for Titus's earlier that afternoon. Dave said in disgust, "That means Steve has been self-medicating. Don't know how or why."

Both doctors quickly took action. They discontinued his IV pain medication and started to flush his system. Steve's breathing became depressed. He went into respiratory arrest. Titus pushed drugs to help increase Steve's lung capacity and Dave intubated him and put Steve on a ventilator. Both doctors continued to flush his system, and slowly his oxygen saturation levels started to rise. Steve started to come around and tried desperately to pull out the intubation tube. Quickly Dave grabbed his arms, and Titus gave him some medication to knock him out immediately. As soon as he got the medication, Steve stopped fighting. "Why don't we leave him intubated for a few more hours? I don't want any surprises."

Dave agreed. Dave stayed with him for the rest of the evening and into the night. It was almost two in the morning, and Dave wrote orders that he was disconnecting the intubation tube. By the time Steve started to come around again, all he had hooked up to him was oxygen, and he was using two liters by nasal cannula. Dave was at his bedside when he woke up. Steve looked away in shame. All Dave could ask was, "Why?"

Steve, still looking away from Dave replied, "Why not? Every woman I've ever dated or for that matter even cared for has either gotten sick, died, or some other catastrophic event has happened. I'm just so tired of letting myself fall for women who are just going to end up dead. So I thought a little more morphine would do the trick. Instead, you, my white knight, came and saved me when I really didn't want to be saved."

Dave could feel anger rising so instead of letting Steve have it, he changed the subject and asked, "Have you remembered anything about the other day in your living room?"

"Bits and pieces have started to come back, but everything is so jumbled. I'm still confused," admitted Steve.

"That's good. Bits and pieces are a start," replied Dave.

"Why did you discontinue everything? My face and head still hurt a lot," asked Steve?

Dave, once again feeling the anger welling up, let some of it go and said, "I can give you an oral pain medication, but I'll not give you the means to try and end your life more than once, not on my watch. You want to try again, you do it on your time, and that's between you and your God."

Steve looked away in embarrassment and finally gave Dave a weak apology. Dave wrote in his chart that pain medication was only to be given as necessary and only as low of a dose possible. Dave left the room and came back in with a couple of pills. He gave them to Steve and he took them. Steve slept through the rest of the night until noon, when he woke with a start.

He was remembering Sarah's husband holding her in front of him and threatening to kill her. He closed his eyes, then had a memory flash of all of them wrestling around, then he remembered the gun going off several times. Steve started to cry. Just then both Titus and Dave entered his room. Dave quickly approached him and tried to comfort him the best he could. Titus did a quick once over and medically he was fine. Steve, through tears, said, "I'm starting to get more of my memory back, and I think I caused Sarah's death. I think I initiated the fight. I was trying to get the gun away from her husband and, if I didn't jump at him, she might still be alive."

"Until you get all of your memories back, you can't second guess your actions. Whatever you did or didn't do, you have to know that your actions were right," replied Dave.

At that point Steve accepted what Dave said, just for the plain fact that he didn't have all the pieces.

Steve spent two more days in the hospital, then was released. As time went on his memory never came back fully. Physically, he was healing. The bruising around his face had lessened and the swelling had almost diminished. Mentally he was still struggling with the loss of Sarah and also with the possibility that he in some way might have contributed to her death. When Steve finally came back to work, both Dave and Titus noticed that mentally he just wasn't the same as before. Dave found Steve in his office, entered and closed the door behind him, and he said, "I've been watching you struggle since you got back. Will you consider going to see a therapist? Dr. Brubaker helped me and my family after Kelly died. You'd like him. He's a no-nonsense type of guy."

At first Steve balked at the idea, but then he continued to think more about what Dave had said, and if he could help Dave and his family after something as awful as Kelly's death, then he could give it a shot. So he made an appointment with Dr. Brubaker and, as it turned out, they both got along great, and he continued to see him for several months. This made a huge difference both in his personal and professional lives, so much that everybody around Steve could clearly see the difference in him.

When Steve saw Dave, he stopped him and said with enthusiasm, "Thank you so much for your recommendation of Dr. Brubaker. Between the two of you, you both saved my life."

"You're welcome. Everybody who works with you and around you has commented to me what a good and positive change you've made," Dave said enthusiastically.

"Once again it's all thanks to you," replied Steve.

Dave smiled widely, and Steve went back to work. After Steve left, Dave breathed a sigh of relief and thought, now I hope Bay County's doctors can settle down and have no drama, but then he laughed out loud and said, "Fat chance of that ever happening."

Then Dave went back to his office to the mounds of paperwork that was piled on top of his desk. He was trying to get some of it under control because he knew that in just a few days he, along with Steve, were going to a medical conference in Utah.

CHAPTER 5

Dave and Steve were running through the busy Utah airport trying to catch their flight. They had just come from a medical conference, and Steve was presenting, and it ran long because all in attendance were asking so many questions about Bay County and its emergency department.

Once to the gate, they found out that they were too late. Their flight to Boston was already pulling away from the gate. Dave asked the young lady at the desk by the gate if there were any other flights out this evening. She quickly typed something into her computer and said to Dave, "The last flight out this evening is leaving from Gate 12, and I've already informed them that you're coming, so please hurry. Gate 12 is located down the corridor and to your left. It's the first gate that you'll come to after the left turn."

Dave thanked her, and once again they both took off running toward Gate 12. When they arrived, Steve glanced at the plane and, out of breath, asked the gentleman at the gate, "Is that our plane?"

"Yes, it's a twelve passenger airplane, and it's dependable," the attendant at the gate said.

"But it's so small!" Steve rolled his eyes at the small plane.

Dave reassured him, and Steve and Dave boarded the plane. As they arrived on board there were already eight passengers on board, and they made ten. They sat next to each other, put their seat belts on, and quickly the plane was pulling away from the gate. Steve was still nervous as they taxied toward their take off. Take off was routine, and Steve seemed to relax somewhat as they continued to fly, Steve seemed more and more relaxed until the pilot told the passengers that there was a storm approaching and the plane may experience some turbulence.

Steve started to freak out and quickly pulled his seatbelt tighter. Dave did the same, but to most of the passengers this didn't seem to bother them. Steve gripped the arm rest so tight that his fingers and knuckles started to turn white. The flight started to get bumpy, then the plane started to rise and fall, then the severe lightning and loud thunder started, Steve's white knuckle flying continued, and he could have pulled that arm rest straight off his seat.

Then a lightning strike flashed, and a loud boom that wasn't thunder sounded. The pilot came on the intercom somewhat out of breath and said, "We just lost an engine to a lightning strike and the closest airport is Denver. Please don't be alarmed. We can still maintain flight with one engine."

Steve gasped, and Dave reassured him that the pilot is well trained and knows what to do in these types of situations. Dave was saying these words and hoping that he was right. He was also scared, but didn't want to show that to Steve.

As the storm raged on, so did the turbulence of the plane. The plane pitched back and forth in violent fits. Then the plane would leap forward and dive down. Then all of a sudden the plane leveled out and the weather outside the plane calmed, both Steve and Dave collectively breathed a sigh of relief. Then out of nowhere a blinding bolt of lightning hit the plane, and the plane pitched upward, then it had a rapid decent. The pilot yelled into the intercom, "All passengers need to brace for a crash landing. We just lost our other engine. We're going down!"

Then the pilot switched the intercom off and made a mayday call to Denver and also back to Utah, but neither airport received that mayday call because the plane was already too low and the mountains were interfering with the signal. Both airports were tracking the plane as it went off the radar, and both airports were already sending out air rescue toward the location where the plane went off the radar.

The pilot did the best he could to try and gentle the decent and slow the plane down so the crash wouldn't be so violent. He did the best he could, but the crash was tremendously violent; in fact, once the plane came to rest, it didn't look much like a plane. The nose and the cockpit had been totally ripped away as were both wings and the tail section. The plane was in pieces and on fire.

Steve and Dave quickly unbuckled themselves and went to all the passengers to get them up and out of the plane. Dave was leading them out of the main cabin door. The emergency shoot didn't deploy, and suddenly Dave realized why, the plane was on its side and at least ten feet from the ground. Dave yelled at Steve over the roar of the fire, "Can't get out this way. Is there any other way out?"

Steve looked toward the back of the plane and realized that there were too many exposed live wires that could electrocute somebody, plus the back of the plane was filling with smoke and was getting hotter by the second. Steve once again yelled at Dave, "No, go at the back of the plane. We're going to have to do something in your direction. That's our only chance!"

"Is there a life-raft on board," asked Dave?

Steve didn't answer, just frantically looked for one. That was when the rear of the plane now had started to burst into flames.

The passengers were screaming, crying, and yelling as they crowded toward the front of the plane. Steve finally found the survivor raft and quickly tied twine from the galley to the raft so that, once they threw it from the plane, they could pull it where they needed it to be. Steve ran to the exit as Dave pulled the cord to inflate the raft, and Dave held onto the twine as he threw it from the plane.

It landed right-side-up, but Dave would have to somehow turn it over so that it would cushion the passengers' fall. They didn't have much time. The smoke and the flames were getting closer. Dave continued to tug on the twine, but it wasn't heavy enough to turn the raft over. Dave knew what he had to do. He needed to be on the ground so he could physically turn the raft over, then hold it in place for the passengers to jump on safely. Dave yelled at Steve who was still in the back of all the passengers, "I'm going to need to get down there and turn the raft over so the rest of the passengers can exit safely. We don't have much time. The plane is going to explode soon."

Steve argued with him, then Dave just stepped out of the plane. He tried to control his landing and land in or on the raft, but that didn't happen, so he landed half on and half off the raft. As soon as he hit the ground with his right foot, he heard and felt both bones snap in his ankle. He screamed in pain and rolled around on the ground, cradling his broken ankle. Then he managed to compose himself, and he crawled over to the raft. He turned it over and held on to it. "Are you okay," asked Steve?

"Broke my ankle. Send the passengers one by one and have them drop on their bottoms and they should be okay."

Steve helped the first passenger to the door with the others looking on in disbelief. The passenger went out of the plane and landed on her butt, and the raft saved her. Seeing this, the rest of the passengers felt better about their escape route. Passenger after passenger safely exited the burning plane. The fire was getting closer to the exit door. Steve was hurrying the passengers as best he could. It was down to him and one other passenger. Steve quickly grabbed blankets and first aid kits from the plane, then told the last passenger besides himself to jump. The man said in a shaky voice, "I'm really scared of heights, and I don't think I can."

"I understand about fears, but your alternative isn't great. You either jump or get burned to death when this part of the plane explodes, which it's going to do any minute."

Steve tried to push the man into the door opening, and he wouldn't have anything to do with that. He fought Steve off, and finally the man begged Steve to go before he did, so Steve jumped out of the burning plane. Once he was on the ground, Steve screamed up to the man and said, "Piece of cake. Now it's your turn. Come on, the plane is about to go up. You need to jump now!"

Steve quickly looked over at Dave, and he was being taken care of by a couple of passengers. Just as Steve looked back up at the plane, the plane exploded. It was a large explosion, knocking everybody close off of their feet. Then a passenger on the ground screamed loudly at the moment all the passengers were looking up. The man who had refused to jump earlier was totally engulfed in flames and fell from the plane.

He hit the raft first, but by the time Steve and another passenger could throw a blanket over him to douse the flames. He was already dead.

Steve didn't uncover the body, but instead asked for the other passenger to help him move the body away from the plane. In fact, all the passengers moved away from the burning wreckage. The rest of the passengers were all horrified at what they had just witnessed. Steve felt bad, but under the circumstances there was nothing he could have done to save that man.

Steve knelt down where Dave was sitting on the ground and asked, "Did you break both bones?"

Dave, who was suffering from the pain, managed to say, "I would assume so. I heard both bones snap as I landed, and it sure feels like it. You're going to need to splint it and try to set the fracture so I can get blood flow back to my foot, so I have a chance to keep my foot."

"That's going to be tough without any sedation," said Steve.

Steve popped up and got one of his light-bulb looks and said to Dave, "Hang on, I'll be right back."

Dave watched him go from passenger to passenger asking them each something, and he managed to get several bottles, then he came back to where Dave was. Steve put all the bottles down beside him and asked, "Here, what's your choice?"

Dave sorted through them, picked up one, and said, "This will do. Don't want to be so wasted that I can't help out."

Steve looked at the bottle now in Dave's hands and said, "Good choice." The drug was Percocet, and Steve said, "Take two now, then I can give you two after we're finished."

Dave didn't hesitate and took two. Steve rolled up Dave's pant leg and went looking for a couple of heavy sticks that would work as a splint. Once he had all his materials, he came back to Dave and asked, "How are you doing now, Dave?"

Dave was starting to slur his words. He was feeling no pain. As he was getting ready to set Dave's ankle, he got one of the male passengers to help him. Steve told the man exactly what he wanted him to do, and the man did exactly as Steve said. The passenger was holding traction just below Dave's knee, and Steve told him that he was going to count to three and try to realign the bones in Dave's ankle.

The man understood and took a good hold of Dave's leg, then Steve counted to three. Steve pulled hard on Dave's ankle and rotated his foot till it was at a ninety degree angle. Dave screamed out in pain even though he had some pain killers in his system. Then Steve asked the man to hold Dave's foot and ankle in the position that he had it so he could quickly splint the ankle. Again the man did exactly as Steve told him to do. After the ankle was splinted, Dave ate two more pills and continued to breathe hard until the pain medication started to kick in. Steve left Dave, who was now in a semi-conscious state, and went to check the other passengers. Steve gathered all of the surviving passengers around him and said, "Everybody, I know we all just experienced something traumatic, but I want to know if anybody is hurt. I and my friend who risked his life to save all of us is also a doctor."

One of the female passengers said, "I have some blood coming from my back, but I can't tell what happened."

Steve quickly grabbed one of the first aid kits and went over to her. Steve examined her back, and it looked like a small piece of metal was embedded between her shoulder blades. It wasn't very deep, and Steve quickly pulled it out and put a bandage on the wound. The woman was grateful.

Then Steve once again addressed the remaining nine passengers. He said, "Tonight we need to stay close by the plane. I wouldn't suggest wandering off in the dark. For all we know we might be on a mountain top or even a ledge. It's warmer closer to the plane, so I suggest we use the warmth to our advantage. Get as comfortable as you can and, if you can, try and get some rest. We've all had a very traumatic evening."

According to Steve's watch, it was one in the morning, so they only had maybe five hours, maybe less till sunrise, and that was good. Steve made sure everybody was settled, then went back to where Dave was lying. He was pale even in the fading light of the fire burning from the plane. "How is your pain level," asked Steve?

"I'm doing okay. I hope the pilot got a mayday signal out before we went down."

Steve took that answer and assumed he was in some pain, but was coping. Steve held onto all the prescriptions given to him in case there was another passenger who needed something. Steve checked Dave's splint and said, "I hope the pilot sent a mayday for all our sakes. Try and get some rest. You may need it come morning."

The passengers all settled down, but not many slept. Steve tried to close his eyes, but saw that passenger that wouldn't jump who was engulfed in flames as he fell to his death. Steve quickly opened his eyes. The fire on the plane was still burning, but the temperature had dropped sharply. He looked at his watch, and it was almost three in the morning. He buttoned his coat around his neck and glanced over at Dave, who had curled up in the fetal position, but wasn't asleep. Steve didn't close his eyes for the remainder of the night. He was glad to see the first light. Hopefully this day would bring their rescue from this awful situation.

As it got brighter, Steve got up and checked on Dave who was actually sleeping, then he went around to the rest of the passengers. Some were still sleeping, and others were awake, but resting. Steve tried to get his bearings and the lay of the land. The passenger who was so helpful to him the night before came up to him and said, "I'm sorry that I didn't introduce myself to you last night, but it was all so traumatic. My name is Ted Wright. I'm a computer programmer in Los Angeles. I was on my way to the Cape area to meet up with my family for vacation."

"Nice to meet you, Ted. I'm Steve Pratt. I'm a doctor at Bay County Hospital, near Boston."

Both men shook hands as the rest of the passengers started getting up and milling around. Steve and Ted gathered them and asked, "Is anybody from this area? We may be in Colorado. We're at a higher elevation, I can feel the pressure, and the air is much thinner."

None of the passengers said anything. Then Steve said, "We can do without food, but we can't do without water. So our first priority is to find water. I want us to pair up and go off into different directions. I want each of the pairs to walk for no more than an hour in the same direction. If you find a source of water, yell. We'll find you. Good luck to all of us."

Before Steve and his partner Ted went off in their direction, he wanted to check on Dave. Dave had made it to a standing position, but when he tried to take a step, he fell into Steve's open arms. Steve laid him down as gently as he could. Steve looked at Dave and said, "You stay put. I'll try to find you a strong branch that you can use as a crutch, but for now stay down."

Then Steve went off, and quickly he was out of sight of Dave. Then Dave was alone next to the burnt-out plane. Every twig that snapped, every bird that chirped, every sound made him jump. He wanted to explore the pieces of the airplane that remained, because maybe there was something inside that may prove useful to them.

Instead of him trying to stand, which didn't work out so well the last time, he decided to crawl to the first piece which was the nose piece. All he found in that section was the charred remains of the pilot. The electronic equipment was also fried. He crawled over to the tail section and managed to look inside. He couldn't tell what was inside it, so he managed to pull himself up and into the tail section. He found in a closet twelve packs of bottled water and twelve packs of varied flavors of soda. He was proud of himself that he was indeed a useful member of this group. Dave managed to drag one of the twelve packs of water and soda out of the tail section and back to their makeshift camp site.

As it got later in the morning and Dave didn't hear any of the passengers yell that they found water, he was becoming discouraged because what he found wouldn't last long. The sun was directly overhead, so Dave figured that it was mid-day and still nobody had yelled. As the sun started to set, the passengers slowly started to come back to the campsite. Then a yell came, and then another yell. It was Steve and his partner Ted. They had found a source for water.

He knew that Steve wouldn't let the other passengers down, and he didn't disappoint. Steve gathered everybody together and said, "There's a stream about ten minutes due east of here. The first time I walked right by it. There's a lot of growth around the stream. The water will need to be boiled, but we do have a steady supply."

"But until we can start hauling water, here's some bottled water for us now," added Dave.

"Did you find that in the tail section?"

Dave nodded and smiled. All the passengers patted Dave on the back. Steve, Ted, and another passenger built a fire, and they all slept much better that night. Steve was still tortured by the man who refused to jump and ended up dying because of that fear, but he didn't let on that anything was bothering him. Steve checked on Dave and his splint and took pulses in his foot and ankle despite a lot of swelling. His pulses were strong both in the ankle and also in the foot. Dave's pain level was also down from the night before.

The next morning they all woke to the sound of a plane. All passengers except Dave immediately jumped up and down and waved their arms widely in hope that the plane would see them. As it passed over, the plane did see them, and the plane dipped its wings to one side, then the other, to signify to the passengers that the plane did in fact see them. "He saw us! The plane saw us!" he yelled.

They all cheered and went back to the campsite. Everybody was excited about being rescued. Then about an hour later a rescue helicopter appeared and all ran back into the clearing. The voice came over the loud speaker and said, "There's no place close for us to safely extract all of you. You'll all have to hike to higher ground. I'll lower food, water, and blankets and a map and a compass. Do you have any injured passengers?"

Steve nodded and put up one finger. The helicopter lowered the supplies, and all of the passengers helped carry everything back to the campsite. The helicopter loud speaker came on again and said, "We'll meet you at the extraction site in two days. Good luck!"

Then the helicopter flew away. Steve quickly looked at the map and realized that it was far, and everybody would have to push themselves for all of them to get to the extraction site in two days. That is, if nothing went wrong during the trek there. Steve went back to the makeshift campsite, gathered the passengers around, and said, "Okay, everybody, you all need to listen and listen good. We have to make it to the extraction site in two days, and it's a far way to go. The terrain looks challenging, to say the least. It's in our best interest to start now. I want each person to carry a blanket and two bottles of water each. If you can carry three, do so."

"What about Dave," asked another passenger?

"Dave is my responsibility. He won't cause us to lose time, I guarantee it. I'll make a carrier, and I'll pull him like you pull somebody on a sled. Ted will be the lead, and Dave and I will bring up the rear and the rest of you will stay in between. We'll leave in an hour."

Steve quickly found two large branches, tied them together at one end and, using the twine from the floatation device, fastened the blankets over the branches, then with the seatbelts from the plane; he got Dave onto the makeshift stretcher and tied it to himself with more seatbelts. Then Steve looked at his watch and an hour was up. Steve said to Ted, "Let's get them going."

The rest of the day was a challenge. The terrain was bumpy, and it wasn't ideal for the makeshift stretcher to travel over, but they both managed to keep up. When it became too dark for Ted to see what was in front of them, they stopped in a small clearing and set up camp. All the passengers were exhausted, but not as much as Steve was. As they both laid there exhausted, Dave said, "Let me use one of the thick branches as a crutch and I'll keep up. That way you're not so worn out."

At first Steve thought this method wasn't the best, but Dave continued to bug him, so he gave in, and they broke up the makeshift stretcher. Steve strapped the extra materials on his back just in case he would need to reassemble the stretcher later. The passengers made a small fire. Everybody was too tired to do much else but sleep. The next morning Steve and Ted met and, using the map, they plotted their course. They had today and tomorrow to get to the extraction site. Both men agreed that they would have to make a lot of miles today. Steve reminded Ted that it was his job to get the passengers to the extraction site regardless of him or Dave. Ted insisted by saying, "If it wasn't for Dave's sacrifice, we'd all have perished when the plane exploded. We'll all make it to the extraction site."

Steve didn't argue with Ted, but instead went back to Dave, who was trying the branch as a crutch. He was doing okay. Steve said to everybody, "Okay, today will be harder than yesterday. We have to make a lot of miles today. Carry what you can, but don't get too weighted down. Let's get our stuff together and, once again, you all will follow Ted, and Dave and I will bring up the rear."

Ted and the rest of the passengers grabbed their stuff and Ted said, "Okay, folks, let's go."

Ted started out due north as they had been going according to the map. At first Dave was keeping up great, but he quickly tired and slowed. Ted stopped the passengers and went to check on Dave. Dave was out of breath and sweating. Steve saw Ted coming and met him and said, "Dave is okay, but it's taking a lot of strength to maneuver this terrain, so I want you to stick with the map we'll follow. No matter how far back we get, you must keep going. Do you understand?"

"Why are we on such a rigorous time schedule," asked Ted?

"That is why." Steve pointed to the skies to the south. They were jet black against the sun to the north. "The chopper pilot stuck a note in the map and told me not to alarm the rest of the passengers, but this storm approaching is going to get bad and we're not equipped to ride it out. So the extraction site is our only hope. Don't say anything to the passengers about the storm. We don't want to panic them anymore than they already are. You need to urge them to pick up the pace."

Ted looked over at Dave, who looked all done in, and Dave said in bursts of breaths, "Don't worry, we'll make it!"

Steve nodded in agreement. "We're about a half day away from the extraction site, but from the look of that sky to our south, we'll have to push to make it to that point before the storm beats us there. One more thing, Ted. Whatever happens, you need to make sure those passengers get on the extraction helicopter regardless of Dave and me. Promise me!"

"I promise, Steve." He hesitated.

Ted took the map and went back to the passengers and told them that they were less than a half day's walk from the extraction site. They were going to have to pick up the pace. The passengers were glad to hear that they were getting closer to being rescued, and that fact only made them get up and follow Ted at an even quicker pace.

Steve and Dave, who were about ten minutes behind the others, Steve quickly checked Dave's ankle which was swollen and red and irritated where the makeshift splint was rubbing on his skin. His pulses were still palpable, which was all Steve could hope for at this point. "Okay, Dave, ready?"

Dave smiled and moaned as he got up and said, "Would it make any difference if I said no?"

Steve shook his head, and with Dave using the thick branch as a crutch and Steve supporting him from the other side, they slowly started off distantly following the rest of the passengers. They continued this way until Steve stumbled, and that caused Dave to fall. He fell awkward and screamed in pain. Steve gathered himself up and quickly went to Dave.

Steve pulled his pant leg up and, to his horror, saw the exposed fibula bone that Dave had broken when he fell. Dave was in a lot of pain. Steve took off the splint and had to try and force the bone back into his ankle. He told Dave to bear down and that it was going to hurt. Dave braced himself, and Steve pushed hard on the bloodied bone and managed to push it back inside.

He then fashioned another splint out of the extra materials that he was carrying on his back. Now that Dave had an exposed wound, he would have to be extra careful about how and where he walked, if he could walk at all.

Steve gave Dave some water and asked, "Do you think you can stand?"

Dave gathered himself and, in much pain, stood shakily. Steve got in front of Dave, ducked down, and said, "Get on my back."

Dave wanted to tell him no, but he knew that this was the only way. The question was how long Steve could carry Dave on his back. Steve, with Dave on his back, moved slowly through the terrain, but continued to move nonetheless.

Ted and the rest of the passengers were less than an hour away from the extraction site when the wind suddenly switched and the temperature dropped about ten degrees in a matter of just a few minutes. Steve also felt the drop, and he tried his best to pick up the pace. His legs were burning and his lungs felt as if they were on fire, but he continued with Dave on his back, which at this point he'd passed out from the pain and blood loss. Steve and Dave were about an hour behind the rest of the passengers, and Steve continued to drudge north. As he did so, the sun went away and the sky clouded up completely. The temperature was in a constant tail spin downward.

Ted and the rest of the passengers actually made it to the extraction site before the helicopter did, but nobody seemed to mind, considering that all of the passengers, including Ted, were exhausted and just glad that they were about to be rescued.

The extraction site was a large clearing that looked like it was used many times before for helicopter landings and take-offs. Ted kept looking back to where they came out of the brush for Steve and Dave. There was no sign of either of them. Then Ted's attention was diverted to the approaching helicopter. All the passengers cheered and clapped and said to Ted that he did a great job leading them to the extraction site. Ted quickly helped the passengers into the helicopter, then asked one of the crewmen on board, "How much longer can we wait? There are still two men back in the brush and one is injured."

The crewman looked at the pilot, and the pilot gave a signal, then the crewman said, "I'm sorry, but we can't wait any longer. The storm is close, and if we don't leave now, we may not make it out period."

Quickly Ted gathered blankets, water, and even a couple of coats, put them against a tree, and weighted it down with several bottles of water and a large rock. Ted said to himself, "Good luck, boys. I hope you both can survive the storm."

Then he ran back to the helicopter and they took off. Once the helicopter made it back to base and they got all of the passengers safe, tended to any of their injuries, and got them settled, Ted asked one of the crewmen, "How long is this storm supposed to last?"

"According to the radar, the storm doesn't look like it will last long, but it'll be hard hitting and will dump maybe a couple of feet of snow," replied the crewman.

"How soon can you go back and search for the two missing passengers?"

"Depends of the wind speeds, but just as soon as the storm passes. Don't worry, we'll find your friends."

Meanwhile, the airline got word from the rescue helicopter and immediately made calls to all the passengers' families. John got the call from the airline. The man from the airline said, "Dr. Dobinson, this is Dan Zimmerman from Utah. I have some information on passenger Dr. Steve Pratt and passenger Dr. Dave Bradfield. I'm sorry to inform you that they didn't make it to the extraction site on time. As far as we know they both are still alive, but there's a storm moving across that area. As soon as the rescue helicopter can get back in the air, they'll continue the search."

John, shocked by what he just was told, asked, "Do you know why they didn't make it to the extraction site? Were they injured?"

"Yes, one of them was injured, but I don't know which one. If you'd like to fly out here, I can arrange it so you can be here as early as tomorrow afternoon," said Mr. Dan Zimmerman.

"Yes, I want to be there!"

Dan gave him the rest of the flight information, and John left a note for his secretary detailing what was happening, then called Dave's home. The new nanny answered. John introduced himself to her and she did the same, then John told her what was happening and she told John that she would stay with the children until further notice. John said to her that he would keep her posted. She wasn't sure what she should tell the children because they thought that their father was coming home in the morning. John told her to tell them that the flight was delayed due to bad weather. She understood and thanked John for calling.

Meanwhile, back near the extraction site, the wind had picked up and the entire sky had turned a mean shade of grey. Steve tried to hurry to the extraction site, but at this point couldn't go any faster than a slow walk. Finally, they made it, and Steve knew that they were too late. He gently put Dave down up against a tree and went to check out what Ted had left him. He saw the note first, and it said that the helicopter would be back as soon as the storm breaks so stay close to the site. Steve smiled, then realized that he had left blankets, coats, water, and a tarp with some twine.

Steve knew that he didn't have long to get a crude shelter set up before this storm was upon them. He went back into the woods where the trees and bushes were denser and put up his crude shelter. The he saw lightning through the trees and heard the thunder. He quickly tied down the last strap of twine and quickly went to get Dave, who at this point was at best semi-conscious.

He half carried, half dragged Dave to the crude shelter and laid him down in one of the corners, covered him with a blanket, and would save the coat for when it got really bad. Steve started a small fire which would help with warmth. The lightning and thunder lasted for a few minutes, the rain started and the temperature fell quickly.

The rain then turned to ice, then the ice quickly turned to snow. The small fire wasn't enough to keep them both warm, and Steve didn't want to risk anything bigger for fear of burning a hole in the top of the plastic tarp. Steve bundled Dave up with another blanket and put the coat and hat on him. Steve put the extra coat on, and both men huddled close to each other so they could share each other's body heat.

Steve couldn't let his guard down because from time to time he would have to get up and knock off the snow from the top of the tarp so it didn't cave in from the weight. The wind had started to let up, but the snow continued to fall fast and furious. After the fourth time getting up and cleaning the snow off the top of the tarp, Steve fell asleep. He woke to a numbing cold. He blinked hard several times to focus and, when he finally did, he realized that the tarp had collapsed on top of them due to the weight.

Steve managed to check Dave, who was alive, but he didn't like the color of his foot and ankle or his pale facial color. Steve managed to crawl out from underneath the tarp that now was almost completely buried by several inches of heavy thick snow. He stood and looked at the dark grey sky and knew that it was going to continue to snow for maybe quite some time.

So this time he cleaned off the snow from the tarp and fashioned more of a lean-to, so the snow would slide off and maybe make somewhat of a barrier from the bitter cold of the conditions outside. After he was finished with the lean-to he started a small fire, and now that it was day, even though the sky was still dark grey, he could examine Dave's foot and lower leg.

The bandage which was a piece of shirt was now soaked through with blood and had pieces of the ground embedded in the bandage. Steve quickly checked pulses above the break and below the break and both were still palpable. Steve threw away the blood-soaked bandage and ripped the bottom of one of the blankets and wrapped it around the open fracture. Dave moaned and became conscious. He looked around and saw Steve and asked, "Guess we didn't make the extraction site in time?"

Steve nodded and gave Dave a bottle of water which had started to freeze slightly. Steve said to Dave, "Here you need to drink. The rescue helicopter knows that we're here and just needs the storm to clear and we'll get out of here."

"The temperature has fallen a lot. You need to stay conscious. How is your leg?"

"I'm just glad it's cold, because the air temperature is acting like an ice pack. My foot and leg is pretty numb, thus the pain level isn't an issue. What time is it?"

Steve looked at his watch and he said, "It's almost eleven in the morning."

Dave peered out the opening of the lean-to and said, "It looks more like six or seven in the evening. Steve said, "We're going to need something to eat. Ted left us water, but no food. I'm going to see what I can find. Your job is to not let our small fire go out and you need to stay awake. I won't be gone long."

Steve got up and stood outside the lean-to and immediately sank down into the snow at least six to eight inches. He knew this wasn't going to be easy. As he began to head away from their shelter, it stopped snowing. He was glad of that. Since he had no gun, he would have to go the roots and berries direction, if he could find any in all of this snow.

When Steve returned, he was surprised that Dave was conscious and he actually had added to the fire. Steve was exhausted and crawled back inside the crude lean-to. He warmed himself by the fire. Then he took out of his pockets pieces of roots and a few berries. He said, "Sorry there isn't more, but the snow has most of the bushes covered."

Steve shoved everything from his pockets over to Dave, and Dave hesitated, then said, "You need to eat as well. Something is better than nothing."

"I ate a few berries as I picked them. These are for you; now eat."

That was a small white lie, but in their current situation Dave needed the few berries worse than he did. Dave ate them and drank most of the bottle of water. Steve was glad to see him eat. He just hoped this storm would soon be over because their meager situation wouldn't last long. Steve, who was exhausted from the hunting and also because he didn't sleep the night before, couldn't manage to hold his eyes open any longer, so Steve asked Dave, "If I rest for a few minutes, can you man the fire?"

"Sure, you rest. You need it since I was unconscious all last night."

Steve curled up close by the fire and quickly fell asleep. Dave knew that Steve shouldn't be sleeping for long. The lean-to was cold, and the fire wasn't that big of a heating element. He waited about twenty minutes, then said to Steve, "Steve, you need to wake up."

Steve didn't move or wake up. Dave yelled louder at Steve, and once again Steve didn't move. Finally, Dave had to physically move closer to Steve and pushed him hard in the back with his hand and said in a loud voice, "Wake up, Steve!"

Steve, groggy, opened his eyes and looked at Dave. Steve said, "Thanks for waking me up."

Steve managed to sit up and peer outside of the lean-to. It had started to snow again, and this time it was the hardest snowfall thus far. Steve added a couple more small twigs to the fire. Dave asked, "How did you learn how to do all this? You grew up in the city, didn't you?"

Steve, who never talked about his childhood said, "Well, for a couple of summers I spent time at a wilderness camp, and it was either learn how to survive or not survive. I chose to survive. Then, when I was older, I was a camp survivalist and helped other young boys learn how to survive in the wilderness. The snow unfortunately was never part of that training. So I'm basically winging it."

"You're keeping me alive, and that's saying something," replied Dave.

Dave's eyelids started to get heavy, and he lay down and rolled over close to the fire and said sleepily, "Quick nap, okay?"

"Only a few minutes," replied Steve.

Dave was asleep before Steve finished his sentence. Without food and much water, Steve knew that in his current state he wouldn't be able to stay awake much longer. After about twenty minutes Steve woke Dave up with a brisk shove and shouted his name. Dave opened his eyes slowly, then blinked hard to get more awake. That continued for the rest of the day and into the night. Finally, Steve knew that neither of them could go on like this any longer. So while Dave was sleeping he piled on more sticks and got close to Dave so that both of them could share body heat. Then Steve fell asleep.

Steve woke up slowly and blinked several times to get his eyes to focus. A person dressed like a doctor was standing in front of him. The doctor urged him to consciousness and said, "Dr. Pratt, you're safe. You're in the Utah State Hospital. Your injuries aren't severe; a little hypothermia and mild dehydration, and I would imagine that you're somewhat still sleep deprived."

Steve asked, "How is Dave? How is his foot?"

The doctor replied, "Dr. Bradfield came through surgery great, I believe it's because of you he'll walk normally again. He'll be on crutches for a while and may need some physical therapy to strengthen his muscles. As soon as he's out of post-op he'll be next to you in the other bed. There's a Dr. Dobinson who has been here, and he'd like to see you. Are you up for it?"

Steve nodded.

The doctor left, and John came into Steve's room with a concerned look and Steve said, "John don't look so concerned. We're both going to be fine."

"Yeah, I know that now, but you weren't on the other end of that phone call that I received a couple of days ago. The representative from the airline told me that you both were missing and that was all he knew. The waiting and the worrying was enough to drive a person crazy," John said.

"You should have been out in the elements and go through a crash of a small airplane. Now that is worrying!"

John sympathized with Steve, then the doors opened to the room and a couple of orderlies wheeled in a semi-conscious Dave.

He had a few minor scrapes, and his foot and lower leg were heavily casted. Quickly after he was moved over from the operating gurney to the bed, he started to become more and more conscious. Steve talked to Dave until he was fully conscious, and John realized what a bond Steve and Dave had. Feeling all warm and fuzzy in the moment, John excused himself and stepped outside leaving Steve and Dave alone. Dave, still fuzzy and disoriented from the anesthesia, blinked hard several times trying to get the cob webs out. Finally everything was clear, and he slowly looked around the room, then he saw Steve in the next bed and whispered to him, "You okay?"

"Yeah, I'm okay. Little exposure and somewhat sleep-deprived, but that's how I'm most any weekend."

Steve asked, "Hey, I've been meaning to ask you, why did you make such a quick decision to jump from the entrance to the plane? You knew that you'd be risking injury."

"Because I knew that if I did get hurt, you'd be the better person in those elements to keep me alive, and I bet right," said Dave.

Steve, shaking his head slowly, replied, "So in that split second decision you bet that I was a better outdoors man than you. Wow! You were really betting against the house."

"No, actually I was betting on a sure thing," said Dave.

They both laughed.

Steve was discharged from the Utah State Hospital the next day, then Dave was discharged a day after. Once they were all back together, Steve asked, "John, please tell me that we're flying home on a commercial flight."

"Is a 747 big enough for you," replied John?

"Yes," Steve said with a huge sigh.

Dave chuckled and so did John, and for once Steve didn't find the humor in them laughing, and that made both John and Dave laugh that much harder.

By the time they got back home to Bay County it was late, and Dave's kids were staying at friends for the past couple of days so the house was empty when they arrived. Dave's foot was throbbing, and Dave asked Steve before he left his house, "Steve, before you leave, could you do me one more favor?"

"Yeah, sure," responded Steve.

"I could really use something for the pain in my foot and ankle," said Dave.

"Sure, just let me get home and I'll fax it to your pharmacy. You won't get it until morning. If that's not soon enough, I can run by the hospital and grab you something for tonight," replied Steve.

Dave thought for a moment, then said, "You know I think I have a couple of Tylenol three with codeine and that'll do me just fine until the morning."

Steve yawned and was getting up and Dave said, "Why don't you stay here tonight? It's already late. I don't think I'm going to venture upstairs. I think I'm where I'm going to stay for the night."

Dave was in the oversized recliner in the living room.

"I think I'll stay since you're so kind to offer. Before I get comfy, can you tell me where you keep the medication you want to take and I'll go get it?"

"It's upstairs in the main bathroom behind the box of Band-Aids."

Steve quickly went up the stairs and searched the medicine cabinet, and sure enough, it was right where Dave said it would be. Steve brought down the bottle, grabbed him a bottle of water from the fridge, and gave the pills and water bottle to Dave. Then both Steve and Dave settled down for the night. "Thank you so much for all that you did for me while we were out in the wilderness."

"You're welcome, but it's nothing that you wouldn't have done for me," replied Steve.

They both slept.

As the weeks and months passed after the crash, Dave saw monumental changes in Steve. He was so much more self-assured. He was confident enough before; he seemed that he just had an extra pep in his step now. But the most important thing of all was that Dave and Steve had become even closer, if that was possible.

CHAPTER 6

Steve to this day hadn't learned how not to be kind without feeling the need to pick up strays. This was one such experience, but that same quality unfortunately also made him a compassionate and wonderful doctor.

Steve had pulled a double and was working on his twenty-fifth hour when Dave found him in radiology sleeping, leaning against a light board. Dave put a hand on Steve's shoulder and said, "Steve, I think the x-ray is upside-down."

Steve turned toward Dave, and he looked tired. His beard was scruffier than usual, and his eyes had a red rim from lack of sleep. Dave asked, "How do you get yourself into these crazy shifts?"

Dave shook his head in disbelief, then a nurse walked into the viewing room in radiology and said to Steve, "You have a patient waiting in exam two."

She handed him the chart with the patient's history and general complaints. "Got to go. Duty calls," said Steve.

Dave asked, "How much longer do you have?"

"Dr. Young is coming in. He should be here anytime, and if I play my cards right, this should be my last patient. Then I have the next eight hours to sleep, then I'm back on for the one to one shift," said Steve.

"No! You got tomorrow off; I'll find somebody to cover for you. I don't want to see you back here until day after tomorrow."

"I love you, Dave!"

"I'm glad somebody does!"

They both left radiology, and Steve went to exam room two. Dave had rounds on the fourth floor.

Steve took a quick glance at the chart that the nurse had handed him earlier. The patient's chief complaint was that of blurred vision, nausea, and severe cramps. Steve entered the exam room and saw an attractive, thin young woman in a lot of discomfort. Steve introduced himself and started to examine the young woman. After a short once over, Steve sat on a stool next to the exam table and asked the patient a number of straight-forward questions. "The chart says that you've been experiencing these symptoms for a couple of days. Are these new?"

The young woman replied in a huff, "If you're implying that I'm bulimic or something like that, you can forget it. I'm normally this thin, and my symptoms aren't from sticking my fingers down my throat!"

Steve apologized, but liked that she was spunky. Then he asked, "Have you eaten anything different lately, had anything around you that's out of the ordinary?"

The young woman replied no to both questions. Steve looked perplexed and said, "I'm going to have the nurse come in and get some blood, then we can see what's going on, but in the meantime I'm going to start an IV and give you some fluids and something for the pain."

The young woman smiled at Steve, and he wrote the orders, and a nurse came back in and followed all of his orders. He even put a rush on the blood work. After about twenty minutes Steve came back into the room with the results from the lab. The young woman was still in some pain, but she had calmed down somewhat. "Well, your blood work tells us that you have an infection, so until we can isolate it, I'm going to admit you, and the infectious disease control unit will isolate the infection. My guess is that came from something you ate."

The young woman thanked him, and a couple of orderlies put her in a wheelchair and wheeled her to the second floor under the care of Dr. Edward Jay, who was the top in his field in the study of infectious disease and their causes.

The young woman thought Steve was attractive and even went so far as to ask the nurse for contact information on Steve. The nurse didn't give her much information. She told her it's a confidentiality situation.

Meanwhile, Dr. Young had come in, and Steve wearily handed the ER over to him. Steve said, "Good night."

"It's eleven in the morning," said Dr. Young, who gave Steve a strange look.

Once home, Steve didn't even bother undressing; he just collapsed on his unmade bed and fell asleep almost immediately. Steve didn't wake until six that night. He felt nasty, so he took a shower and was hungry, so he ordered a pizza and turned on the television.

Back in the hospital Dr. Jay found that it was indeed food poisoning causing the young woman's symptoms. He gave her intravenous antibiotics and another round of an anti-nausea medication and a low dose pain killer, and by the next morning she was symptom-free and feeling much better. Dr. Jay discharged her and gave her a prescription for an oral antibiotic. He told her to be careful of her diet for a few days, then gradually eat what she could tolerate. The young woman thanked him and asked, "Dr. Jay, can you tell me how to get in touch with the doctor I saw in the emergency room? I want to thank him for taking such good care of me."

Dr. Jay thought that was a weird request but said to her, "Dr. Pratt saw you when you came into the emergency room, and you can leave him a note at the ER desk, but I don't know his work schedule. You might talk to one of the nurses down in the ER they could tell you more."

She smiled, and Dr. Jay discharged her, then left the room. She was already obsessed over him; in her mind they had already started a relationship. She was so excited to maybe be able to see him again before she left the hospital, but then she was terribly disappointed when the ER nurse told her that Steve wasn't working today. The young woman left a message for Steve, nothing personal; she didn't want to set off any alarms at this early stage. In her mind she was already planning the wedding.

She left the message and, when Steve came in the next day, Connie gave him the message. Steve opened the note and read it. It read, "Dr. Pratt, thank you for taking good care of me. I was released today and would like to buy you a cup of coffee," and she signed her name Anita Compton, then she put her cell number underneath her name. Steve smiled, closed the note, and put it in his pocket. He had every intention of calling Anita that day but the ER got busy. There was a wedding party that invaded the ER that had food poisoning. There were all kinds of wedding party people throwing up and getting sick in trash cans. The staff was hustling to get these people under some type of order.

When everything seemed to settle down, it was too late to call Anita, and Steve had every intention of calling her. So the next morning Steve made it a point to call Anita before he went to work. Anita answered the phone on the second ring; she knew it was Steve because she had caller identification. She tried to calm herself as she answered the phone. "Anita, hi, this is Dr. Pratt from Bay County. How are you feeling?"

"I'm doing much better thanks to your great care," replied Anita.

"I read your note, and yes, I'd very much like to have coffee with you," said Steve.

Anita tried to calm herself, but wanted to fly through the phone and attach herself to Steve. Anita chose her words carefully as she replied, "That would be wonderful. Your schedule is much more demanding than mine. You name the time and the place and I'll be there."

She hoped that didn't sound as desperate as it came out. Steve replied, "How about ten tomorrow morning at Café Mocha on Third and Central, which is near the hospital?"

Anita paused as not to sound too immediate, and she replied, "That'll be fine. I'll see you there."

They both hung up. Steve got ready to work, and Anita began to obsess about everything from what to wear to what she was going to talk about. She was way out of control. She took an antidepressant and had to sit and rest on the couch. She couldn't afford another mental break, not now when she was going to marry a doctor.

After a long night for Anita, it was finally time for Steve and her to meet at Café Mocha. Steve, who wasn't thinking very much about this meeting, came pretty much dressed as usual, which were jeans, polo shirt, and flip-flops. Anita, on the other hand, was business casual. She had on a short black skirt, a short sleeved sweater, and a lavender color shell underneath, and some very smart black wedge shoes that tied the outfit all together. Steve entered the coffee shop and saw that she was already sitting at a table near the large windows. He approached the table and said, "Anita, you're looking much better than the last time I saw you."

Steve sat down and a waiter came over, and they both ordered. "Dr. Pratt, I just wanted you to know that you treated me with dignity and respect. Most doctors who see me always think that I try to be this way. Unfortunately, this is my body type no matter what I do."

"Yeah, I almost went there myself, then when I was taking your pulse I noticed your bone structure in your wrist and knew that you were telling the truth," said Steve.

"Enough talk about me. How long have you been practicing medicine," asked Anita?

"About fifteen years, and six of those are here at Bay County," Steve said with a smile.

Anita wanted to keep asking questions, but knew not to go too far too quickly. Their coffee came, and they both sipped on their cup and chatted for a while longer about the weather and some light politics. Then Steve said something that would turn Anita's world upside down. Steve said, "I just want to clarify something with you, Anita. I agreed to meet you for coffee because you wanted to thank me, and I thought that was sweet, but I make it a policy not to date patients whom I've treated."

Steve finished his coffee, looked at his watch, and said, "Thank you, Anita, for the coffee. I'm late for my shift. I hope you continue to be well."

Steve left the coffee house before Anita could even say a word. She was so surprised and shocked that if her jaw dropped any lower it would be on the table. She gathered herself, managed to pay for the coffee, and left. She went back to her place, tore off her clothes, and completely tore her apartment to pieces. Before she could stop herself, her apartment was almost completely destroyed. She was out of breath and crying.

When she finally calmed down, it took most of the evening and way into the night before her place looked livable again. She sat down and would have to devise a plan to win back Dr. Pratt's affection. She thought on this subject for the rest of the night and into the morning hours of the next day. She finally came to a realization that if Dr. Pratt wouldn't be a willing participant, she would have to show him what he was missing.

She went into her bathroom and loaded a syringe with Ketamine hydrochloride, which was used in veterinary medicine as an anesthetic, and she got dressed and went to put her plan into motion. The Ketamine was left over from her short time at the animal clinic that she worked at a few years ago. Anita had already followed him from work to home a couple of times, so she knew his habits. Anita waited for Steve to get off work and followed him to his house. Steve drove into his driveway, and Anita was right behind him. She honked at him from her car, and he approached her car and was surprised that it was her. Steve said, "Anita, hi."

Steve leaned into the car window and, before he could say anything else, Anita with quick speed pulled the syringe out and injected it into the side of Steve's neck. Steve staggered forward in shock, then slumped over into the open window. Anita put the car in park, slid out of the driver's side, and with great difficulty managed to push and shove Steve until he was in her car. Then she continued to shove and push him until he was in the passenger side.

Exhausted and out of breath, she drove back to her place. By the time she got to her apartment, Steve was starting to regain some consciousness enough to sort of stumble as Anita managed to struggle to get him to her apartment. Once inside, she got him to her bedroom and onto her bed. Anita hurried to the medicine cabinet and quickly came back with another syringe of the drug.

Steve tried to fight her off, but in his current drugged state he was no match for her, and she injected him with the drug and he suddenly went limp. Anita quickly handcuffed him to her bed and went to change into the appropriate clothes for when he became conscious enough to participate in what she had dreamed and fantasized about since she first laid eyes on him.

It seemed like she had to wait a lot longer with him than the others before Steve was aware enough to participate, but not too aware. Anita came into her bedroom, and Steve blinked several times, but still couldn't focus on what was going on. Steve tried to move and realized that his arms and legs were all tied up, and he still couldn't focus on what was going on.

Steve couldn't even talk at this time. All he did was mumble. Anita was ready; she sat on the bed next to Steve and stroked his hair, then seductively started to remove his shirt, then his jeans. The drug was now starting to wear off, and Steve became more aware of his surroundings just as Anita was on top of him. He felt himself get hard, then felt a wave of nausea and turned his head and tried to roll to one side, but Anita was still on top of him so he had no choice and threw-up on himself and Anita. She was so mad that he had done that, but it got her off him and he could sort of turn to his side, and he continued to throw-up.

Anita went into her bathroom to clean up and get more of the drug. This time Steve was very much aware and fought her as much as he could, considering that he was handcuffed to the bedposts and his legs were tied to the bed post and he was naked. Anita, despite the thrashing around he was doing, managed to inject him with the drug and once again he fell silent. She cleaned him up, covered herself and Steve up, went into the bathroom, and took a shower. After her shower she once again was ready to have sex with Steve, which in her mind he was a willing and mutual partner.

Anita once again began to stroke him and kiss him, and again she was quickly on top of him, but this time Steve wasn't aware of any sexual activity on his part. In fact, he wasn't even conscious. She was rough with him and even at one point Steve moaned in pain. She finally dismounted him and was exhausted trying, but to no avail. She had given him too much of the drug. Then she had a frightening thought. What if he overdoses and she would have to call 911? Because, after all, she couldn't let her fiancée die. She couldn't understand that the drug was to get Steve in the mood, and it had worked on others before; why wasn't it working on Steve?

Then Steve started to seize. Anita's greatest fears were coming to realization. She quickly un-cuffed him, untied his legs, and put his underwear and jeans back on him, dragged him into the living room, and called 911. She would have to quickly make up with some story about her date, Steve having a seizure. Anita knew once the ambulance got there, she would be pretty much busted, but the alternative was to let Steve die, and that was something she could not live with. Anita would play the helpful girlfriend as long as she could.

At first the EMT's didn't recognize Steve, but quickly they did realize that the patient was Dr. Pratt, and both technicians became suspicious of Anita and her story. She told the EMT's that they were on the couch in a romantic interlude when Dr. Pratt suddenly stopped what he was doing and rolled off the couch and began seizing.

One of the technicians continued to question Anita while the other EMT gave Steve medication to stop the seizure, and finally the seizure activity stopped. With all the rushing around the EMT's were doing Anita slipped out of the apartment. She would disappear until the heat simmered down. Then maybe she could return and continue the relationship with Steve.

The EMT's stabilized Steve and loaded him into the truck. They rushed him to Bay County and into the trauma room. Dave and Titus met Steve and the EMT's at the door, and they gave Dave the information on Steve's condition as they rolled him into the trauma room. Dave noticed the restraint marks on Steve's wrists and ankles. Dave made sure that the marks were documented, in case the police may get involved down the road.

They rushed his blood work to the lab, and Dave and Titus ran every neurological test. Thus far they all were coming back clean. Now they were just waiting for Steve's blood work. Finally when the lab work came back Dave literally grabbed the paper from the lab technician who brought it up to the trauma room. Dave quickly read through the paper. There was only one drug that shouldn't be in his system, and that was Ketamine.

The large dosage made everybody look twice at the paper. No wonder Steve was seizing. Dave thought how is Steve still functioning, breathing, and living? Dave yelled at the trauma staff, "I need everybody's attention. This patient has overdosed on Ketamine. We need to counteract as quickly as possible, and we're possibly looking at multi-system failures and maybe more seizures. Let's move, people. This one we need to save."

All the nurses and doctors involved in the trauma moved quickly to try and counteract the drug's effects. The team was successful. Steve's vital signs started to stabilize, but he hadn't regained consciousness. Dave was being cautious and ordered another full neurological scan. Dave worried until the scan came back clean. He moved Steve to the intensive care unit for the next twenty-four hours just as a precaution. Dave finished up with the trauma team, then went to be with Steve in the ICU.

Meanwhile, an undercover unit was watching Anita's apartment in hope of her coming back so they could arrest her on multiple charges, but the one question they were interested in was where was she getting the Ketamine? Anita was watching the undercover unit watching her apartment so she knew that she couldn't go back there. She was curious about Steve's condition, but didn't dare go near the hospital for fear it was being watched as well.

Steve was starting to come around after about five hours of being in the intensive care unit. Dave was by his bedside when he started to regain consciousness. He blinked hard several times, then coughed and tried to speak. Dave stood by his bedside and calmed him and said, "Don't try and speak; just rest."

Steve shook his head no and cleared his throat more forcefully. Steve could only manage a raspy sound and said, "It was one of my patients, Anita. I can't remember her last name. The best I can remember is that she thought we were in love. She drugged me and tied me to the bedposts. She's nuts!"

"The police know about the situation and are still looking for Anita," said Dave.

"Everything is still such a blur," replied Steve.

"She used Ketamine to sedate you and confuse you. She finally gave you too much and you started to seize. At least she had somewhat of a conscience and called 911."

"I'm glad she did. I remember feeling sick all the time she had me."

"I have to ask you, did she rape you? We found some heavy bruising on and around your genitals. We're going to have to start you on the standard medication protocol, and you'll need to be tested for HIV once the Ketamine has cleared your system."

Steve closed his eyes and flashed back and remembered bits and pieces of his captivity, then reopened his eyes and said, "Yes, she raped me. I'm only getting bits and pieces, but I remember feeling aroused and not being able to control myself. It was horrible. It seemed like a bad dream. If somebody tells you it would be fun to be tied up, that person has never been tied up against their will."

"Okay, Steve, that's enough for now. I want you to get some rest; we can talk more in the morning," replied Dave softly.

"How long are you going to keep me in ICU," asked Steve?

"I want to make sure that the Ketamine is leaving your system and there are no complications from the drug. Can you remember how much was given to you and how often?"

Steve, with somewhat of a confused look, shook his head no in response. Dave told him that it was okay and he left the ICU room. Even with some light sedation Steve had a hard time settling down. Flashes of his captivity kept surfacing. As this continued, his heart rate started to increase, then his heart monitor went off and a crash team was quickly in the room with Dave not too far behind. Steve was semi-conscious and moaning. Dave got closer to Steve's bedside and asked, "What's wrong, Steve?"

Steve in short bursts, replied, "My chest hurts, feels tight. It's hard to breath."

Dave studied the Steve's monitor, then gave orders for medications, and the crash team quickly carried out the orders. Shortly after the crash team pushed the medication. Steve's heart monitor stopped beeping; his breathing also started to slow and he regained full consciousness. Dave started some oxygen as well. Dave reassured Steve and said, "We're going to start an Isuprel drip and see if that will take care of your heart racing like that."

Steve asked, "Is this from the Ketamine?"

Dave nodded. Steve closed his eyes and slept with the combination of the mild sedative and the Isuprel drip which literally knocked him out. When Steve regained consciousness again, Dave was at his bedside. Dave said, "Good afternoon."

Steve gave a half-hearted smile back to Dave, cleared his throat, and managed to say, "It felt like I slept in a deep freezer."

"It's the combination of the sedative and the Isuprel drip. Besides that feeling, how are you doing," asked Dave?

"Okay, my head hurts and my stomach hurts," replied Steve.

Dave got that serious look on his face and asked Steve, "How does your stomach hurt?"

Steve again cleared his throat and answered Dave, "There's some pain, but mainly I feel nauseated."

Dave quickly checked his urine output. It was almost non-existent. Steve started to get sick, and Dave held the basin while he threw up. The vomit smelled like waste, so Dave knew that his kidneys were shutting down. After Steve was finished vomiting he called Dr. James Ayers, the best renal doctor and surgeon anywhere. Dave quickly filled him in on the phone, and Dr. Ayers told Dave that he'd be down to see Steve in about twenty minutes, but he told Dave that he wanted an MRI and a kidney output test. Dave made note of that in his chart and hung up the phone.

Dave did the kidney function test himself, then the orderlies took Steve for an MRI. When Dr. Ayers came in to see Steve, both tests were there waiting for him to evaluate Steve. Dr. Ayers looked at both tests and wasn't encouraged by either. He made a few notes in Steve's chart, then examined Steve, then said to him, "Since you're a doctor, I'm going to give it to you straight. It's bad; your MRI shows some scarring on both kidneys and the function tests on both kidneys, are at thirty percent. I want you to start dialysis now and hopefully the damage is reversible and the dialysis won't be permanent."

"When will you know, Dr. Ayers, if the damage is permanent or not," asked Dave?

"Let's let the dialysis work for a couple of days, then I can reevaluate your kidney function at that time. Then we can discuss our next course of treatment. A nurse will be in soon to get you prepared for dialysis. Do you have any questions for me?"

Steve, still shook up from the news about dialysis shook his head no. Dr. Ayers left, and Dave was going to follow him out. Steve stopped him and said to Dave, "Can you stay for just a minute, Dave?"

Dave noticed the look on Steve's face and remained at Steve's bedside. Steve said, "I'm scared. What happens if the kidney situation is irreversible? My medical career is over, all because I felt sorry for a patient who ended up being a total whack job!"

Dave patted him on his shoulder and said, "I'd be surprised if you weren't scared. Dr. Ayers is one of the best. Let him treat you, and we can worry about things as they happen or not happen."

A couple of nurses came in and prepared him for his dialysis treatment. They looked at the veins in his arms and decided to go with a central line at the subclavian area. The nurse who started the line was good, her first try, and there was almost no pain.

Then an orderly came in with a portable dialysis machine, and the nurse who started the line also hooked him to the machine. Then she said, "Okay, Dr. Pratt, you're all set. I'll be back throughout the treatment to check on you. Your treatment time will be roughly two hours."

Steve thanked her and she left his room. About every fifteen to thirty minutes she came back and checked on Steve. The two hours didn't seem so bad with her checking on him regularly. Steve had never had dialysis, but was told by other patients that the aftermath of the treatment was rough.

Steve was now experiencing the after effects first-hand. It was beyond rough; it was like doing a cardio-workout for a week straight. He was physically exhausted. He could do nothing but sleep. Dave came in, and Steve was sleeping. He took Steve's chart and read through the chart. Dave was amazed that the treatment had taken that much out of him.

He was scheduled to do another treatment this afternoon, but his blood pressure was down and his temperature was up. Dave called Dr. Ayers and told him about Steve's condition, and Dr. Ayers said, "Dave that is a typical reaction of a patient who first starts treatment."

Dr. Ayers wanted Steve to continue the treatment on time and prescribed wide spectrum antibiotics to help with the fever and also told Dave to up his volume. Dave understood Dr. Ayers's instructions. The nurse came back in and started his second treatment.

This time Steve made it about halfway through the treatment and he started to throw up. The nurse helped him calm down and worked his way through his treatment. Dave came in and gave him some Compazine to help with the vomiting. Again, Steve was wiped out after the treatment and slept and ignored his meals. Dave came in and made him eat, even though Steve was barely coherent, but thanks to Dave he did eat some. Steve was asleep as soon as Dave was finished helping him eat. Steve slept all night and into the next morning. Dave was there to feed him breakfast, and he was again barely coherent.

A nurse came in and gave him some medication through his IV, then got him ready to start his dialysis treatment. After his treatment he was again wiped out, but he was a lot more coherent than the day before. Dave was glad to see Steve being more alert; he ate and drank relatively well. He complained over how bad the food was, and Dave knew that he was doing better. "I'm glad to see you among the living. The first couple of days I wasn't sure that you were going to make it," said Dave.

"I'm just like a Timex; I take a beating and keep on ticking."

Steve managed to smile and Dave laughed. Dr. Ayers came in and had Steve's chart in hand and said, "Okay, Steve, I have good news and not so good news. What do you want first?"

"Give me the good news first," replied Steve.

"I have your latest kidney function tests. They look promising. I believe the dialysis treatment is working, so maybe just another couple of treatments."

"So what's the not so good news?"

"The excessive amount of Ketamine that you were given is now causing calcium deposits around your heart and also in your kidneys. I had first thought that the dialysis would help lessen the amount, but instead it's only moved it around. We're going to have to monitor you closely, and I'm starting you on beta-blockers and blood thinners so you hopefully don't stroke or have a massive coronary. If these medications don't resolve the calcium, we may have to operate and remove the excess calcium by hand, but that's a last resort situation. The drugs should work. We're going to keep you here in the ICU until we can get the calcium levels down. The calcium levels should start to drop quickly once the beta blockers and blood thinners kick in. I'll repeat your CBC in another twenty-four hours."

"That's wonderful, Dr. Ayers. So I possibly have to look forward to stroke or a massive MI, wow! What a situation. Do your thing Dr. Ayers. So far you're batting a thousand with me and my care, so onward and upward," said Steve.

"I'm glad to see you're feeling better and that your sense of humor has come back," replied Dr. Ayers.

"It's either the humor or me crying all the time, and nobody wants to see that," said Steve with a smile.

"Try to keep your chin up and we'll take it one day at a time."

Dr. Ayers left, and Dave remained. Steve looked at Dave with a frantic look. Steve said quietly, "Dave, I don't know how much more I can take."

Dave came over to his bedside, put a hand on his shoulder, and said, "Hang in there, Steve. The drugs that Dr. Ayers is going to give you will clear up the calcium. Be patient; relax. For once, just be a patient instead of a doctor."

A nurse came in and started the beta blockers and blood thinner medications. After the nurse was finished, Dave looked at Steve's chart, then at Steve. "What?"

"I just wanted to make sure that we're still giving you Compazine, because the beta blockers can cause dizziness and stomach problems."

Steve just shook his head, then said, "Dave I really screwed up this time. My feeling sorry for strays is going to wind up killing me, literally. In your opinion, what are my chances of coming out of this still able to call myself a doctor? Please, be honest!"

"Barring any more serious complications, I believe you're going to be just fine and you can keep the doctor that's in front of your name," said Dave.

Steve smiled and breathed a small sigh of relief. The drugs given to Steve earlier were now starting to affect him. He was dizzy and his chest felt heavy. He closed his eyes, and Dave left the room. Steve slept until the dialysis team came in to hook him up to the machine. As the nurse cleaned his central line he moaned and was incoherent. The nurse noted that in his chart and looked for signs of infection from the central line, but there was no sign of any infection, so she continued to get him ready for his treatment.

His treatment was about halfway finished when Steve's heart monitor went off. He was tachycardic at 180 and his blood pressure was down. The code team was called to Steve's room. Dave heard the page, ran to the stairwell, and took the stairs two and three at a time. He was out of breath by the time he got to Steve's room in the ICU.

The code team was pushing drugs, then shocked Steve. Steve's heart monitor went back to a normal sinus rhythm. Dave let out a large sigh of relief as Steve went back into sinus rhythm, and he asked the doctor with the code team, "What happened?"

"Steve was about halfway finished with his dialysis treatment when he became tachycardic, and we defibrillated him successfully into sinus rhythm."

Dave thanked him, and the code team left Steve's intensive care room. Dave sat by his bedside and looked closely back over his chart. Something jumped out at him almost like it hit him in his face. He called Dr. Ayers and told him that it was an emergency, and he came quickly. Dave shared the last code with him, then said, "I know why Steve has a calcium problem. Yes, it's related to the overdose of Ketamine, but when he first was in the emergency room, we gave him a large dose of vitamin B and that, in combination with everything else, helped add to his calcium problem."

Dr. Ayers was amazed at Dave's discovery and asked, "Okay, so how do we solve this problem without Steve dying?"

"It's not the most orthodox way, but I'm going to say it anyway. We take him to the operating room, put him under, stop all medications, put him on the cardiac by-pass machine, and run all of his blood through the filter, then take him off by-pass and hopefully that'll be the fix that we're looking for," replied Dave.

Dr. Ayers thought about what Dave had just told him and said, "I think your plan just might work, but there are some serious problems that could arise from this procedure."

"Yeah, I know. I thought about all of them, and none of them are pretty. I know he could die, but I believe Steve is young and in good health, and he'll survive this. I'm going to bring this to Steve and make sure he knows all the risks, including death. I'd like you to be there as an impartial witness when I tell him," replied Dave.

Dr. Ayers asked, "Sure. Do you want to do that now?"

"Yes, before I lose my nerve," replied Dave.

Dr. Ayers smiled at Dave, and they both walked into Steve's room. Steve was just coming around from his latest heart related episode. Steve asked, "My chest feels like somebody stomped on it. What's going on?"

"You had another tachycardic episode. I want to talk to you about a possible treatment that may end up fixing most of your problems, but I'm not going to lie to you. It could just as well kill you as cure you," replied Dave.

Steve said, "So tell me already. Anything has to be better than continuing to suffer cardiac events until one will be my last."

"This isn't the most orthodox method. We want to stop all medications, then take you to the operating room and put you under, then put you on the cardiac by-pass machine and run all your blood through a high powered purifier filter, then put all of your clean blood back, then take you back off of by-pass and hopefully that'll cure your condition," said Dave.

"So what are you waiting for? Let's get this done," said Steve.

"Wait a minute, Steve. You know better than anybody in this room that at best this is only a guess that could kill you. You need to think about this," said Dr. Ayers.

"If Dave thinks it's going to work, then that's all of a guarantee I need," replied Steve.

Dr. Ayers handed him a blank form with a signature line at the bottom and gave it to Steve. Steve quickly signed it and he left, then Steve asked, "What's next?"

"We'll do the procedure in forty-eight hours, but I have to take you off all medications. I'm afraid it's going to be a long couple of days, but I'll be right here by your side," said Dave.

Dave discontinued all the medication that Steve was on. It took Steve another couple of hours to react, and he became violently ill. Dave held his head while he threw up. Steve threw up for a long time and his breathing became labored, so Dave started Steve on four liters of oxygen. Dave continued by his bedside and said, "Hang on, Steve, you can make it through this!"

Dave had the crash cart parked right outside Steve's room just in case, but luckily it wasn't necessary. Steve slept on and off throughout the rest of the night. On the other hand Dave got little to no sleep. The next morning, Dave got up and left Steve's ICU room, and left specific instructions not to give him any medication, and that he wanted a nurse in his room until he returned. The nurse understood and went into Steve's room. Dave headed to his office and did some research on what he was proposing to Steve. In theory he thought it would work; now he wanted some hard facts that would back that theory up.

He searched and searched and finally found what he was looking for. He studied the research and went so far as to call the doctor listed and talked to him. Dave filled that doctor in on what he was about to do. The doctor agreed with Dave and thought it would work. Dave was grateful to the doctor, and the doctor wished him good luck.

Dave checked on a few of his patients, then went back to the intensive care unit and stayed with Steve. He threw up some more, but managed to sleep on and off throughout the rest of the day and into the evening. Finally, about two in the morning, Dave thought he was sleeping, but he was actually unconscious and his heart monitor suddenly went off. He was once again tachycardic at almost 200, so Dave grabbed the crash cart and, instead of pushing drugs that would slow down his heart rate, he defibrillated him and there was no conversion, so he reset the machine for a higher rate and defibrillated him again. Steve finally converted into a regular rhythm. Dave breathed a sigh of relief and left the crash cart in his room. Dave dozed on and off for the rest of the evening and into the late night hours. Steve didn't regain consciousness for the rest of that time.

The next morning finally came, and Dave left Steve with a couple of surgical nurses who were getting him ready for surgery. Dave needed to wake up because he needed to be on his toes for this. This was a matter of life and death, and not for just some random patient. This was Steve, his best friend. He grabbed a cup of coffee, went into the doctor's lounge, and took a quick lukewarm shower, which brought him to his full senses. Dave got out of the shower, put on a fresh pair of scrubs, went into the wash room, and scrubbed for the operation. Dave was extremely nervous.

He knew that this was risky at best, but he felt somewhat better about things since he talked with the doctor who had done a similar procedure and hoped it would be a success. After he was finished scrubbing, he took a deep breath and entered the operating room. Steve was already prepped and ready for anesthesia. Dave said to Dr. Lee, who was the anesthesiologist whom Dave had worked with for many years, "Okay, Dr. Lee, do your magic."

Dr. Lee went to work, and a few minutes later he said to Dave, "Okay, your majesty, the patient is all yours."

Dave opened Steve's chest as if he was doing any other thoracic surgery. He was assisted by Dr. Ayers and his regular surgical team. Dave was going slow and being deliberate so as not to make any mistakes. Dave finally got Steve hooked up to the by-pass machine and put the special filter in place. He knew from his research that it would take about seven minutes for Steve's blood to run through the machine and filter, then run back into his body. The clock started, and everybody watched the clock.

"How is he doing," asked Dr. Ayers?

"So far, Steve's doing okay," replied Dave.

The seven minutes seemed to crawl by, but finally the time ended. As Dave was disconnecting the by-pass machine, Dr. Lee spoke up and said, "Dr. Dave, he's starting to have Premature Ventricular Contraction, or PVCs, so you need to hurry. I've given him medication, but it hasn't helped."

"I just need a few more minutes," replied Dave.

Dave worked quickly. He managed to get Steve disconnected and started to close when Dr. Lee's voice boomed over the operating room, "He's gone into full arrest, I've pushed epinephrine. You need to start compressions!"

Dave stopped what he was doing and quickly started compressions. The nurse said to Dave, "Internal paddles are ready, doctor."

Dave grabbed the paddles from the nurse, put them on either side of Steve's heart, and Dave yelled, "Clear!"

All who were working on Steve took their hands off, and Dave pushed the button and Steve's heart defibrillated, but there was no conversion. Dave replaced the paddles on Steve's heart and told the nurse to turn the setting to 400.

Dave yelled clear, and all took their hands off Steve. Dave pushed the button. Steve's heart once again defibrillated, but this time his heart converted into a normal rhythm. From there everybody worked quickly to get Steve off the table, because nobody wanted that to happen again.

They got Steve off the operating table alive, but nobody knew for sure if the procedure worked. Dave knew that they couldn't test his blood for another twenty-four hours after the procedure. Everybody involved with Steve's operation was anxious to get those tests done.

Dave joined Steve in recovery and waited for him to come out of the anesthesia. When he didn't respond after a few hours, Dave was concerned about possible neurological problems because of how long compressions had been performed.

From recovery Steve was moved to a surgical intensive care unit room, and he still hadn't regained consciousness. So Dave ordered a Computerized Axial Tomography or a CAT scan to make sure there was no brain damage and also ordered an Electroencephalogram or an EEG, which recorded electric activity in the brain.

Later that same afternoon Dave got Steve's CAT scan and EEG back, and both were normal. That was a big load off Dave's mind, but the question still remained why hadn't Steve regained consciousness?

Dave continued Steve's bedside vigil. For the rest of the night and into the early morning Steve remained unconscious.

Today was the day that Steve's blood work would be drawn and could be analyzed to see if the procedure worked. A lab technician came in and drew Steve's blood. Dave, who was dozing in the chair next to his bed, said without opening his eyes, "I need a complete blood workup, and see if you can rush that."

The lab technician replied, "I'll do my best, Dr. Bradfield."

It was late in the afternoon, and Dave was dozing in the same chair he'd been in since Steve had come out of surgery when Steve said hoarsely, "Dave?"

Dave quickly popped to his feet and was immediately at his bedside and said, "I'm right here, Steve. You had the procedure yesterday; your blood work is being analyzed to see if the procedure worked. I was concerned with you; you didn't regain consciousness until just now. I did a CAT scan and an EEG just to make sure everything was okay. Both tests came back clear. We're now waiting on your blood work to come back to see if the procedure worked. It should be back anytime now."

Just as he finished that sentence Dr. Ayers walked in with a big funny grin on his face. Both Steve and Dave looked at each other, and Dave said, "Let me guess, Dr. Ayers, the procedure was a success."

"Yes, there still is a trace of the Ketamine and calcium but the majority of the drug is gone. I can't believe it worked. Steve, you have one smart doctor in Dave. You should be glad that he works here," said Dr. Ayers.

"Don't worry, Dr. Ayers, I thank God for Dave every single day. This isn't the first time he's saved me," replied Steve.

"Steve has had his share of saving me as well," replied Dave.

"That's beautiful, you all," said Dr. Ayers.

Dr. Ayers left, and Dave and Steve looked at each and laughed at Dr. Ayers comment.

On the last day Steve was in the hospital something much unexpected happened. Anita walked into Steve's room and stood in front of him. At the time Steve was dozing. When he woke to find Anita in front of him, he immediately pressed the nurse call button. Steve quickly gathered himself and said, "Anita, I wondered where you had gone. You disappeared so quickly that I didn't have time to thank you for saving my life."

Anita smiled. A nurse poked her head in, saw Anita, and quickly ducked out and went to call security and Dave. Dave arrived first and entered Steve's room. Steve looked scared, but under control. "Oh, Dr. Pratt, I didn't know you had company."

"Yes, this is Anita Compton. I was just thanking her for saving my life," said Steve.

Dave looked at Anita, and she was beaming with the praise that Steve was giving her. Dave was ready for anything, but really wanted security to come and arrest Anita and take her away. Then Anita raised her right hand, and Steve realized that she had a scalpel. Dave saw the scalpel as well and froze in his tracks. Steve kept talking to her in hope that he could talk her into dropping the scalpel. "Anita, till now, you haven't done anything foolish. Do the right thing here and drop the scalpel."

"Foolish? That's been my whole world; you, my darling doctor, have made me see the errors of my ways. Just remember I'll be the best lover you'll ever have!"

Steve was slowly getting out of bed, and Anita slowly raised the scalpel. Steve yelled at her, and Dave lunged at Anita, but not before she slit her own throat. Both doctors lowered her to the floor, and it only took a few minutes for her to bleed out despite both Steve and Dave applying pressure. She died without saying anything else.

Finally, security came into Steve's room and was shocked to see Anita dead on the floor, and both Dave and Steve covered in her blood. Dave looked up in disgust and said as the security guards entered, "Now you show up. Your services aren't needed any longer, but you can get the coroner up here as soon as possible."

The security guards holstered their guns and left the room. One radioed for the coroner to come to Steve's room. Dave helped Steve out of bed and said, "You ready to get out of here?"

Steve, staring at Anita's dead body replied, "I sure am."

Dave got him a clean pair of scrubs, and Steve changed. Dave and Steve walked out of the room, and each of them knew just how lucky Steve was and that this whole situation could have turned out much worse.

CHAPTER 7

After the whole incident with Anita, Dave thought that a change of scenery would do Steve good, so he sent him to the medical conference in Washington, DC. At first Steve wasn't too keen on going, but he realized that Dave wasn't going to change his mind. So he rolled his eyes at Dave and said, "Okay, whatever. Where and when do I go?"

Dave smiled a large cheesy smile and said, "I knew you'd see it my way." He handed him a pamphlet, airline tickets, and a hotel voucher. He grabbed the information out of Dave's hand, looked at it, and said, "I guess, since the board is picking up the bill, I'll consider this a working vacation."

Steve attended the conference, and it was so boring, but he had to keep reminding himself that he wasn't picking up this bill the fat cats on the board were. So he had plans to eat at the steak house that evening, and he enjoyed every bit of the dinner. Since the whole Anita-stalker situation he had learned to enjoy everything just a little more. He went to his room full and satisfied.

On the second day of the conference Steve heard a speaker on triage techniques, and the speaker grabbed his attention. After the lecture Steve went to talk more with the speaker. Steve walked up to the speaker and introduced himself. "My name is Dr. Steve Pratt. I'm from Bay County, and I'd like to speak with you more on your triage plan."

"Hey, I'm Dr. Richard Sampson, and I've heard about you and your emergency room. I'd love to talk with you more, but I have another presentation in ten minutes. How about breakfast in the morning, say around nine?"

"That sounds great; I'll meet you in the restaurant," replied Steve.

Steve decided to attend another lecture, then he would go out and see the sights. After sight-seeing he went back to his room and studied Dr. Sampson's method and outlined several questions for him to answer at breakfast tomorrow. Steve ordered room service so he could continue to research Sampson's triage method.

In the morning Steve got ready, grabbed his notes, and went down for breakfast. Dr. Sampson was at a table near the windows. Steve sat opposite of Dr. Sampson. A waitress came and took their drink order, then went away.

"I do have a few comments and questions for you about your triage system," said Steve.

Dr. Sampson said, "Okay, fire away!"

Steve looked at his sheet, then back up at Dr. Sampson and said, "First, since we're a smaller hospital, can your system be adapted for my emergency room?"

"Yes. I can send you the specifics on how to set-up and maintain the triage system for an ER like yours. If I may ask, how do you triage now?"

"It might seem old fashioned to you, but it seems to work for us. When a patient walks into our ER, we have two nurses up front at the desk. They ask the patient what's wrong, then another nurse takes them back behind the desk and gets a quick check of vitals, then they're labeled a specific color that relates to their illness, an example of this is a green patient would be a sore throat etc. The next rating is yellow and that would be a high fever, bleeding, etc. Yellow is more emergent than green, but still non-life threatening. Then the last rating is red, and that would be something that is or could be life-threatening. Then we see and treat the patients in accordance to their color," said Steve.

Dr. Sampson replied, "For the most part that's what my system is all about, but just brought into the computer age."

Steve asked, "What do you charge for your system?"

"You're going to think I'm crazy, but here goes. If you put me on staff, the program comes along for the ride," said Dr. Sampson.

Steve said, "I thought you said you were at West Side Hospital."

"I'm sorry if I misled you. I'm employed by West Side; all I'm doing is selling my system. All I really want to do is practice medicine. After all, I'm a doctor, not a salesman," said Dr. Sampson.

Steve was shocked and wasn't sure what to say. Finally he asked, "What's your specialty?"

"I was trained as a thoracic surgeon, but have worked in the ER and also general surgery," said Dr. Sampson.

"As tempting as it would be for me to say yes, I'm not the one who hires and fires. Our Head of Medicine is John Dobinson, and I know that he's a fair and level headed doctor. He would consider your situation," replied Steve.

Dr. Sampson asked, "Next week I'm going to be in your area. Do you mind if I come in and bring Dr. Dobinson my resume`?"

"Sure, I think it would be great to have you on staff," said Steve.

Dr. Sampson thanked Steve, and they made small talk for the rest of breakfast. Shortly after Dr. Sampson was finished, he excused himself and told Steve that he had another presentation to give, and he also told Steve that he paid for breakfast. Steve thanked him, and Dr. Sampson left the restaurant. Steve finished his food, then sat there in disbelief.

Steve went back to his room and googled Dr. Sampson. For the most part the information consisted mainly about his triage system. He did find one link that only talked about his medical career. As Steve read his career, it seemed wonderful. He started in Chicago as a thoracic specialist, then went to Los-Angeles and started implementing his triage system. Then West Side Hospital hired him to get the program, then they put him out on the selling circuit. Steve was blown away by his credentials, but wondered why he wanted to come to Bay County of all places.

Steve was due to fly home later that afternoon. He was glad to be going home. Once home, Steve called Dave and talked about his encounter with Dr. Sampson. Dave had heard of him and wondered the same thing; why did he want to come to Bay County? "I wasn't sure either, but Dr. Sampson is coming to Bay County sometime this coming week. Can you talk with John about this situation? I think it would be great to have him on staff," said Steve.

"I'll talk with John and I'll see you tomorrow," replied Dave.

Once back at work, Steve could talk of nothing else but Dr. Sampson and his triage system. By mid-day all who were working with Steve were sick of hearing about Dr. Sampson and his triage system.

On Wednesday morning of that same week, in walked Dr. Sampson. He came into the ER and asked the triage nurse if he could see Dr. Pratt. She asked who he was, and immediately Dr. Sampson introduced himself. She got up and went to find Steve. Steve came out with the nurse and was shocked to see Dr. Sampson as they both shook hands with each other and exchanged hellos. "Hey, Dr. Pratt, can you direct me to Dr. Dobinson's office?"

"Let's not be so formal. My name is Steve."

"Great, that suits me just fine. My name is Richard, but my friends call me Rich."

Steve said to the triage nurse, "I'm going to take Rich up to Dr. Dobinson's office. I'll be right back."

The triage nurse nodded, and both doctors walked toward the elevators, Steve took him up to the fourth floor and down the hallway to John's office. Steve knocked on the door and from inside John said, "Come in."

Steve and Rich entered his office, and Steve made the introductions, then Steve left them alone. John got up from behind his desk and both men shook hands. "Please, Dr. Sampson sit down."

Dr. Sampson sat down and handed John his resume`. John put it down on his desk without looking at it. John said, "I'm very aware of your credentials, Dr. Sampson."

"Please call me Rich."

Dave asked, "Why do you want to be on staff her at Bay County, when you've worked at some of the most well-known hospitals in the United States?"

Rich replied, "Because I don't want to be a salesman anymore. All I want to do is practice medicine, and get back to the one on one patient-doctor relationship."

Dave asked, "I understand that, but why here?"

Rich leaned forward in his chair and said, "I've kept tabs on this hospital. I know about how well this hospital works and how important it is to the community and the surrounding area. Like I said before, I just want to practice medicine again."

Dave asked, "So what's your specialty?"

"I was trained in thoracic surgery, but have also done emergency medicine and general surgery," replied Rich.

"Okay, Dr. Sampson, Rich; I have to take this to the board. Is there a contact number for you?"

"My cell is 202-263-8201; I'll be in town for the next two days, then off to Washington State for yet another seminar," replied Rich.

John said, "I'll try to have an answer for you before you leave town."

Both John and Rich stood and shook hands, and Rich left his office. He made his way back downstairs and back to the ER. Rich once again asked for Steve, but this time was told that he was with a patient, so Rich wrote down his cell phone number and asked the nurse if she would give it to Dr. Pratt. Then he left the hospital.

Several hours later Steve got Rich's message and called him. They arranged to meet for drinks and dinner.

Dave stopped by John's office and wondered what his thought was about Dr. Sampson. John said, "I think he would be an asset to our hospital, but before I take it to the board, I want to talk to some of the doctors whom he had worked for in the past. If everything checks out, then I think I'm going to offer him a position in general surgery and, with his background in thoracic, he could help you and Steve both."

Then John asked, "Why does he want to come here to Bay County?"

"He's heard how well our hospital works and how important it is to the community. He just wants to practice medicine again," said Dave.

Dave's pager went off and he said to John, "I'm due in surgery. Let me know what's decided."

Dave left John's office, and John immediately got on the phone and called Dr. Sampson's previous hospitals. Everybody he talked with had nothing but great things to say about Dr. Sampson's ability and overall demeanor with patients. John was pleasantly surprised to hear such good things and was much more at ease in recommending Dr. Sampson to the board.

In the meantime, Steve and Rich met for drinks and dinner at a local restaurant. They talked mainly shop, but did manage a little personal information. Rich told him that he was married, but it was a messy divorce, and they had had no contact with each other for a long time. Steve shared that he hadn't had a serious relationship, but hadn't had time for anything serious. Both agreed and finished dinner. Rich told him that he needed to get up early to get to his seminar in Silverbird. Steve took him back to his hotel, and Steve said, "I hope everything goes okay because I think that you'd be a great asset to Bay County."

Rich thanked him for the compliments, shook Steve's hand, and went into his hotel.

The next morning John would meet with the board and would make his recommendations to hire Dr. Sampson. For once, the board accepted John's recommendation and officially put Dr. Sampson on staff. John immediately called Dr. Sampson, who was in the middle of his seminar, so he let the call go to voice mail. John called down to the ER and wanted to talk with Steve. The nurse handed Steve the phone and John said, "I want to thank you for recommending Dr. Sampson be put on staff. The board went along with that recommendation, so again thank you for that."

"That's good news. It'll be good to have an extra hand around here," said Steve.

John asked, "Can you pass the news on to Dave? And ask Dave if he could set a schedule for him and get him set up with human resources. I'm going out of town tomorrow."

"Sure, I'll pass on the information," replied Steve.

The conversation ended, and Steve quickly called Dave and told him the news and also filled him in on that he was going to handle his schedule. Dave wasn't surprised that John let him handle getting him set up.

John got a call, and it was Dr. Sampson. John gave him the good news. Rich was excited, and John said to him that if he came in tomorrow, Dave would get him settled. Rich understood and told John thanks and hung up his phone.

Dave, looking at his schedule to see what time he had tomorrow to get Rich settled, called Dr. Sampson. Rich answered and Dave asked,

"Dr. Sampson, I'd like you to come in tomorrow at nine in the morning for your physical and get you set up with a schedule and with human resources."

Dr. Sampson told Dave that he'd be there.

Steve was in a treatment room finishing up with a patient who had just been diagnosed with diabetes and was having some issues with his blood sugar, so Steve was trying to educate him on how and when he should be testing his blood. Dave came down and caught Steve coming out of that treatment room. Dave said, "Steve, Dr. Sampson is coming in at nine tomorrow morning for his physical and drug test, then we'll set him up with human resources and a schedule. Can you do the physical and drug test for me, then I'll meet you in your office and I'll take care of the rest."

"Sure, that will be no problem," replied Steve.

The next morning Dr. Sampson arrived, and Steve gave him his physical and drug test. Then Steve took him to his office, and Dave was waiting for them. From there Dave gave him a quick tour of the hospital, and after they were finished he sent him down to the human resources department, and they got him set up with a badge and he filled out forms so he could get paid. Rich went back up to Dave's office, and they had a question and answer period. Dave gave him a tentative schedule, then right in the middle of them talking; Steve called and asked if they both could come down to the ER. There had been a house fire and they were getting the family out and getting ready to transport the family.

"We'll be right down," replied Dave.

Rich looked at Dave, and Dave put the phone down and looked at him and said, "Looks like you're going to get your feet wet sooner than you thought. Steve just called and there's been a house fire. A family of three is being brought in. You ready?"

"I was born ready to practice medicine," Rich replied excitedly.

Both doctors went down to the ER, met up with Steve, and Steve filled them in further on what was coming in. There were two ambulances coming in together. "Okay, Dave, you take the first with the father, and Rich and I will take the mother and the young child."

Dave took the father to Trauma room 2 and worked him up. His injuries were extensive, and he had second degree burns on the upper part of his body and numerous broken bones and internal injuries. Dave managed to stabilize him enough to get him up to the operating room, where a surgeon was standing by. Dave located Rich and went in just as he was pronouncing the mother. "Anything I can do to help?"

Rich asked, "Yeah, what's your process for after I pronounce a patient?"

"Here, I'll take care of it. Why don't you see if you can help Steve? He had the young child," replied Dave.

Dave stepped into the room and finished what Rich had started. Rich went to find Steve. Steve was working on the child, and his injuries weren't life-threatening. He had some smoke inhalation and a possible broken right tibia and fibula. Steve was in the process of getting radiology to come and shoot pictures of the leg. As Steve looked up he saw Rich. Steve motioned for him to come in. "What's the status on the rest of the family?"

Rich replied, "I had the mother, and she didn't make it. Her injuries were too severe for her to survive. The father I believe is in surgery as we speak."

The young boy started to come around, and Rich moved closer and comforted the boy and told him that he was going to be okay. Steve liked his bedside manner and that he was aggressive without being intrusive.

Once Steve and Rich were finished with the boy, they admitted him to orthopedics and from there a doctor would set and cast his leg. Both doctors walked out of the treatment room and Dave met them in the hallway. "Sorry that your first patient died."

"I am, too, but on a happier note, its' wonderful interacting and treating patients again. I was afraid I'd be rusty, but it turns out that it's just like riding a bike. Once you learn how, you never forget."

Dave and Steve smiled, and Steve's stomach growled loud enough for the others to hear. Rich smiled, then laughed. "Sounds like we missed lunch?"

"Yeah, but you need to know that the only thing that's more aggressive than Steve is his stomach. We have local eateries that will deliver. So since you're the newbie, you pick. It doesn't matter; your choices are sub-type sandwiches, Chinese, pizza, or burgers," said Dave.

Rich said smiling, "Man, way to put the new guy under the gun. I don't care; how about pizza?"

Dave nodded in agreement and said to both Rich and Steve, "I'll order it. Meet me in my office in about twenty minutes."

Both doctors nodded at Dave, and he went off toward the elevators. "Do you have a place to live yet?"

Rich shook his head no and Steve replied, "Why don't you stay with me and maybe tomorrow when I'm off we can go hunting. Do you want a house or would you rather rent an apartment?"

Rich thought for a moment, then said, "If possible, I'd like to look at houses. I anticipate being here for a long time. This is such a perfect fit, I can't imagine being anyplace else."

Steve said with a smile, "Just wait until you've been here for a while. This place grows on you over time. You're in good company, and we're alike in our thinking about Bay County."

Rich smiled at Steve, looked at his watch, and said to Steve, "We better get you and your stomach up to Dave's office."

Both doctors walked to the elevators, went to the fourth floor, and entered Dave's office. They all sat down, and the pizza delivery man had just come. They all ate and mainly talked shop, Rich continued to ask questions about the hospital and about procedures.

After they were finished, Dave looked at Rich and said, "Dr. Sampson, you're not officially on duty, so if I were you, I'd get out of here while you can. You'll soon find out that this hospital is like a vortex. It'll suck you in, and it's difficult to break free."

Rich snickered at his analogy, finished his pizza, and went back to Human Resources, picked up his ID, and left the hospital. He drove around town so he could get his boundaries.

For the next few days and even the rest of that first month Dr. Sampson was gung-ho. Through time, some of that attitude wore off, but it was evident that he was a great doctor and an excellent surgeon, and he fit into the Bay County family like he'd been here his whole career. For Dr. Sampson, Rich to those he worked with, it all boiled down to the patient-doctor relationship and to make that relationship last well beyond the walls of the hospital.

CHAPTER 8

D r. Richard Sampson had only been at Bay County for just a few months and already he was making a name for himself, but this was the wrong type of attention, especially since Rich had just gotten back into practicing medicine.

Rich was right in the middle of a messy wrongful death suit involving a patient whom Rich treated, then died. The family members thought that he should have had major surgery instead of a less invasive procedure that was performed successfully. Steve had already testified about the patient's condition and treatment. Steve had to testify because he treated the patient in question when he came into the emergency room. Rich was up next. Dave was in the courtroom more for moral support. He had a vested interest in the hospital, and he didn't want anyone to give his hospital a bad name. Dave and Steve tried to give Rich advice, but he was too upset to listen.

The night before Rich was supposed to testify he spent most of it going over Walter Reed's medical file. By doing this he felt somewhat prepared, but was still extremely nervous.

The morning came quickly, and he only managed to get a few hours of sleep. He showered, shaved, put on his best suit and tie, and drove to the court house.

Once at the courthouse Rich met with his lawyer, and his lawyer gave him some directions. They both went into the courtroom. Dave was in the gallery for support today as he had been from the start of these proceedings. This made Rich feel somewhat better that the hospital actually supported him.

The judge came into the courtroom and everybody rose, then everybody was seated. Rich's lawyer, Mr. Reynolds, rose and called Rich to the stand. He was sworn in and took a seat in the witness box.

Mr. Reynolds addressed the court and Rich by saying, "Dr. Sampson, your fellow doctors have testified earlier about the medical treatment given to the patient Walter Reed. Can you tell the court what your role was in Mr. Reed's care?"

Rich cleared his voice and began to speak, "After Dr. Pratt had done the angiography, which is a catheter that's inserted in an artery, and with Mr. Reed we went in through his groin. The catheter is threaded into the coronary artery. Special dye, which can be seen on an x-ray, is injected through the catheter. Then x-rays are taken as the dye flows through the coronary arteries, which outlines blockages and tells the doctor the location and extent of the blockage. It was clear to all the doctors involved that Mr. Reed had three of his major arteries 90% blocked. Thus, Dr. Pratt and I both agreed that an angioplasty would be the procedure and also the procedure that was less invasive."

Mr. Reynolds asked Rich, "Okay, Dr. Sampson, so you've just established that your patient, Mr. Reed, needed an angioplasty. So can you explain for the court what an angioplasty procedure is?"

Rich replied, "It's where we insert another catheter with a balloon on its tip and it's directed to the arteries that are blocked. The balloon is then expanded which pushes the plaque against the artery wall, relieving the blockage, and that in turn improves blood flow."

Mr. Reynolds asked, "How long does this procedure take?"

"This procedure is non-invasive, and it's usually done with minimal sedation, and it usually takes between forty-five minutes and an hour, depending on how many arteries are blocked," said Rich.

"Dr. Sampson, what was Mr. Reed's condition during the procedure and after the procedure?"

Rich again took a deep breath and replied, "He was in critical condition, but his vital signs were stable, and he remained in that condition during and after the procedure."

Mr. Reynolds asked, "Can you tell the court, Dr. Sampson, what happened next?"

"After the procedure, Mr. Reed was placed in the Cardiac Care Unit where he would get intensive care around the clock. I made sure he was settled, then I started to make my rounds, checking on a couple of my other patients when I got a 911 page from the CCU. I hurried to the unit where I found the code team performing CPR on Mr. Reed. The head of the code team quickly filled me in on Mr. Reed's condition. He told me that Mr. Reed had developed an arrhythmia and had to be defibrillated, but with no success. I jumped into the code team's action and pushed several drugs all of which were meant to start the heart beating. None of the drugs worked. I defibrillated Mr. Reed twice more, but there was no response. I then called time of death. The nurses and the code team disconnected the machines and started to prepare the body for the coroner," said Rich.

Mr. Reynolds asked, "Do you believe you did everything within your medical powers to try and save Mr. Reed?"

"Yes."

Mr. Reynolds said to the court, "No more witnesses, your honor. We rest our case."

The judge looked at his watch, then said, "Let us take a fifteen minute break, then when we return I'll be your turn, Mr. Rothingberger, to cross-examine Dr. Sampson."

During the break Rich met with his lawyer and also quickly visited Dave. Dave told him that he was doing a great job and that meant a lot to him. After the fifteen minute break, court reconvened. The judge reminded everybody that they were still under oath. Rich took his seat next to Mr. Reynolds, and they whispered to each other until Mr. Rothingberger stood up and addressed the court. "Your honor, I'd like to call back to the stand Dr. Sampson."

Rich got up and sat in the witness box. Once he was seated, Mr. Rothingberger asked, "Dr. Sampson is there not another procedure or surgery that could have been performed?"

Rich replied, "Yes, there's a more invasive procedure which is by-pass surgery, which essentially is open heart surgery."

Mr. Rothingberger asked, "Why wasn't by-pass an option for Mr. Reed?"

"In most cases, doctors try the less invasive procedures first to clear the arteries, then if needed by-pass is performed. In Mr. Reed's case he wouldn't have survived the surgery. He was not strong enough," answered Rich.

Mr. Rothingberger asked, "When performing the angioplasty, can't the catheter cause heart muscle damage?"

Rich, disgruntled at what Mr. Rothingberger said, Rich replied somewhat forcefully, "No, not if the catheter is in the proper and capable hands of a skilled surgeon."

Mr. Rothingberger said, "Speaking of capable hands, besides being a Bay County for the last several months, when was the last time you practiced medicine?"

Mr. Reynolds quickly stood and objected and said, "Your honor, I object. Dr. Sampson's qualifications as a doctor aren't on trial. The fact is that he holds a physician's license in good standing with no complaints against him."

The judge said, "Mr. Rothingberger, you know better. Do you have anymore questions that pertain to the case?"

"Sorry, your honor, and yes, I just have a couple more," said Mr. Rothingberger.

"Continue, Mr. Rothingberger, carefully," said the judge.

"Was there an autopsy performed?"

"Yes, I believe there was," replied Rich.

Mr. Rothingberger handed Rich a lengthy document and told him, "Can you please read the highlighted portions on page twelve."

Again Rich's lawyer sprang from his seat and said, "Your honor, this document wasn't in evidence. My client has never seen this document before."

The judge asked, "Mr. Rothingberger, what's this document and why have you not shown it to Mr. Reynolds or his client?"

"Your honor, there was no time. The coroner just handed me this document right before court today. Your honor, all it contains is cause of death and documented findings from the autopsy," said Mr. Rothingberger.

"I'll allow it, Mr. Rothingberger, but tread lightly," replied the judge.

Rich quickly glanced at the document, but couldn't read quickly enough to know what it said before he had to read it out loud. He read, "According to the Bay County coroner, the cause of death was a massive Myocardial Infarction, which in turn caused muscle death, which caused the patient's death."

The last section highlighted Rich did read quickly enough before he read it out loud. He totally disagreed with what it said. Rich continued to read from the document, "Under coroner's notes it states that by-pass would have been a better choice, if the patient could have tolerated the surgery."

Mr. Rothingberger took the document back. Rich asked the judge, "Your honor, can I respond to the last statement that I read?"

The judge asked, "Mr. Rothingberger, do you have any objections to Dr. Sampson responding to what he just read?"

Mr. Rothingberger's face got red and he said, "No, your honor, I guess not."

"The coroner could not have known what procedure or surgery would or would not have saved him. I had to make that call at the time, and I believe that he would have never survived the by-pass. At the time I went with what made sense," said Rich.

"Anything else, Mr. Rothingberger?" asked the judge.

"No, your honor, we rest our case," said Mr. Rothingberger.

The judge said, "Since this case is my sole responsibility, I want some time to make sure I have all the facts in order. Court will adjourn for the day, and I'll have my ruling tomorrow morning at nine a.m."

The judge banged his gavel and all rose and waited for the judge to leave. Dave went up to Rich and told him that he thought that he had the case won. "If you don't mind, I'll wait for the judge to tell me that. No disrespect to you, Dave."

"None taken, Rich. I totally understand," replied Dave.

They walked out of the court room and Rich asked Dave, "I'd really like to work today."

"It's okay with me. Tell Steve that you're his for as long as you want to work. Don't get roped into anything you don't want to do, because Steve is a master at manipulation," said Dave.

Rich smiled and thanked Dave. Rich quickly went home and changed, then went to the hospital. Rich told Steve that he really needed to work, and Dave told him that it was okay. Steve understood and gave him a patient's chart, and Rich took it and went into treatment room three. When Rich entered the room, according to the chart, it was supposed to be a twelve-year-old boy with breathing complications. What Rich saw was a large obese child struggling to breathe. He went into the treatment room and, before he did anything, he put the boy on four liters of oxygen by nasal cannula, which settled him down enough that he could talk to the boy and get to the bottom of what was causing his condition. His mother was there with him, and she was overweight as well.

Rich spent a long time on this case. He gave the boy some breathing treatments and also gave him a couple of prescriptions, one for an inhaler and another script was some steroid medication to help with the inflammation. Rich was being as tactful as he could and said, "Your symptoms are going to get worse if your weight goes any higher. There's a good pediatric nutritionist who's right here at the hospital, and she would be glad to see you."

Rich held out her card for the boy to take, but the mother snatched it and asked, "Are you finished, doctor?"

Rich got the message loud and clear. He said, "Yes, ma'am, I'm finished."

Both the boy and his mother waddled out of the treatment room and out of the hospital. Rich put the chart at the nurse's station and picked up another. He walked into exam room two and found a middle aged man curled up in a fetal position. Rich positioned himself where he could see the man's face. Rich said, "Hi, I'm Dr. Sampson. How can I help you, Mr. Peterson?"

Mr. Peterson spoke in short, painful bursts, "I was at work this morning. My stomach wasn't feeling right, upset, and I threw up, which immediately made me feel better. About thirty minutes later in the middle of the board meeting I got the most painful cramps that I have ever had in my whole life."

Rich asked, "Have you eaten anything different in the past twenty-four hours?"

"No, I'm picky about what I eat and where I eat it. Last night I had pasta primavera. I cooked it myself. Everything was fresh ingredients from the farmers market on Eighth Street."

Rich asked again, "Have you taken any new medication or supplements that you haven't taken before?"

"No," replied Mr. Peterson.

"I'm going to do some blood work, then we can get a clearer picture of what is causing your discomfort," said Rich.

Mr. Peterson asked, "In the meantime can I get something for the pain?"

Rich replied, "If you could, wait until after the blood test, so we can see what's going on, then I'll know how to treat your condition appropriately. Once we draw your blood, it shouldn't take too long for the lab to come back with the results."

Rich stepped out of the room went to the nearest computer and put in Mr. Peterson's M.O. to see if he was in the system as a drug seeker. Sure enough, his name came up; in fact, about half a dozen aliases popped up, but his picture matched. Steve was just coming out of another room, and Rich called Steve over and pointed at the computer screen. Steve said, "Print this out and give a copy to your patient. Put a copy in his folder and put on his folder in large letters DS on the outside of the chart and send him on his way. If he gives you any grief, call 2100 which is security."

Steve went away and Rich went back into Mr. Peterson's room and did just as he was told. Mr. Peterson sat up and became angry. He came quickly off the exam table, which took Rich much by surprise and started beating on him. A nurse came in, saw what was going on, and quickly called security. Security came in quickly and handcuffed the patient, and the nurse went to see about Rich. Rich was conscious and trying to get up off the floor. With the help of the nurse Rich managed to get off the floor. Rich was disoriented and dizzy. The nurse sat him down in a chair and went quickly to get Steve.

Steve took one look at Rich, grabbed the phone in the exam room, and ordered a full skull series. Once that was ordered, Steve examined Rich and checked to see if anything was broken. His nose felt like it was broken, and he had a cut on his right cheekbone that was going to need stitches. His right eye was already starting to swell shut. Steve took him to radiology, and the full skull series was negative. All it showed was that broken nose, nothing else. When Steve got Rich back to the exam room, he stitched the cut on his cheekbone, set his nose, gave him a couple of ice packs, and asked if he wanted any pain medication.

Rich replied, holding the ice packs to his face with a grimace, "I wish. I'm due back in court in the morning."

"Okay, make sure you keep the ice on your face. You're going to be swollen and black and blue. You're going to look like hell, but you should be able to make it through court," said Steve.

Rich shook his head in disbelief and with his ice packs left the hospital. The next morning when Dave saw Rich in court he couldn't believe what he looked like. Dave approached Rich and asked, "What happened to you?"

"A drug seeker didn't want to leave the ER without drugs. I found him out and he took me by surprise and got the better of me," replied Rich.

Rich's whole right side of his face was swelled and black and blue. When Mr. Reynolds saw him, he couldn't believe his eyes. Rich quickly explained to his lawyer what happened.

The judge came in and everybody stood, then the judge was seated and he started by saying, "Dr. Sampson, will you please rise." The judge looked at Dr. Sampson and asked, "Doctor, are you going to be okay?"

"Yes, your honor. Just a hazard of my job," replied Rich.

The judge said, "I've gone over all the evidence, and I find that Dr. Sampson did everything within his powers to try and save Mr. Reed. This case is dismissed."

Rich breathed a loud sigh of relief and thanked his lawyer and Dave for his support through this whole trial. "I hope you don't mind if I take a couple of days. My face hurts!"

"That's fine; I was going to suggest that you take a couple of days anyway. I hope your face feels better," said Dave.

Everybody went their separate ways. The next couple of days Rich relaxed and recovered and, when he returned to work, his face looked better. Most of the swelling was gone and the bruising was lighter. Rich was on-call on the surgical floor, but he had no surgeries planned. Rich was sitting at the nurse's desk getting caught up on his paperwork when he received a page from the ER. He grabbed the phone and dialed 7303, which was the front desk of the ER. The nurse picked up the phone and said, "ER nurse Molly."

"Hey, Molly, this is Dr. Sampson. Did somebody page me?"

"Yes, we have a patient who came in and wanted to speak with you. He said that he saw you the other day. He's in treatment room three," said Molly.

"Okay, Molly, I'll be right down," replied Rich.

When Rich got down to the ER, Molly was waiting with the chart. Rich took the chart from her and looked at the notes to re-familiarize him with the case. Then he went into the treatment room. The same twelve-year-old obese boy sat before him. "Dr. Sampson, I want to see the doctor that you gave to my mom. I'm tired of being fat, and I don't want to die early."

Rich asked, "So I guess this is without your parent consent?"

The boy asked, "Is that going to be a problem?"

Rich asked, "Is there anybody besides your mom who can sign a consent form for you?"

The boy thought about it for a minute, then said, "I have an older brother. He is twenty. Can he sign the form? Please, doctor, I'm scared for my life!"

Rich thought long and hard and finally said, "I want your mother on board with this, so I'm going to tell you no, not until your mom signs off on the consent form."

The boy was dejected and started getting his stuff together. Rich called after the boy, "I have another option. Can I call your mom and, if she gives me verbal consent on the phone, then you'd be set."

The boy's spirit's lifted and he said, "She may go for that, just as long as she doesn't have to do anything," replied the boy.

Rich asked, "Is this the right number?"

The boy nodded and Rich stepped out of the room and called the boy's mother. At first the boy's mother was dead set against the idea, but then Rich filled her in on her obligations, which were none. She gave her consent, and Rich thanked her and hung up the phone. He went back into the treatment room and told the boy the good news. The boy was so excited to hear the good news, but his face went sad and Rich asked, "What?"

The boy asked, "How am I going to make it to the appointments?"

Rich replied, "No problem. Can you make it here?"

"Yes, I only live about three blocks away."

"Then there's no problem. Her office is here at the hospital."

Then the boy smiled and was happy, and for the first time he felt hopeful about the future. Rich showed him to Karen's office and introduced him. "Dr. Zimmerman, this is Rudy Anderson and he has his mother's consent. He'd like your help to lose weight."

Karen Zimmerman smiled at Rudy and looked sideways at Rich and said, "Rudy, you know once you enter this program it'll be a lot of hard work."

Rudy replied, "I know Dr. Zimmerman, I'm ready not to be fat. I want to live a long and healthy life, and at this rate I'm afraid that I won't live very long."

Dr. Zimmerman was impressed with Rudy and his honesty, and she looked at Rich, then at Rudy, and said, "Mr. Anderson, I believe I have room for you in my program."

"Okay, Rudy, if you need anything, don't hesitate to let me know. I'll let you both get better acquainted," said Rich.

Rudy replied, "Thanks for everything, Dr. Sampson."

Rich went back upstairs to the surgical floor and continued to work on the mound of paperwork in front of him.

The weeks passed, then months, and Rich became more and more a permanent fixture at Bay County. Then suddenly and without warning a woman from Rich's past showed up at the hospital.

She stopped at the emergency entrance and asked where she could find Dr. Sampson. The nurse picked up the phone and asked whoever she was talking with the location of Dr. Sampson. The voice on the other end told the nurse that Dr. Sampson was in surgery for most of the morning. The nurse put down the phone and said to the lady standing in front of her, "Miss, Dr. Sampson is in surgery for most of the morning. Can I give him a message and he can get back with you later?"

"No, no message. I will try back at a later date," She said.

She turned around and left the hospital. Later that same day Rich came down to the ER, and the nurse told him about his lady visitor from earlier that morning. Rich got defensive and asked, "What did she look like?"

"She was medium height with reddish blonde hair. She was dressed business professional."

Rich quickly thanked her and disappeared upstairs. He now had an office that's on the fourth floor. Rich went into his office and sulked. From the description that's given by the nurse it sounded like his x-wife, and it was an extremely messy divorce. As he remembered, the police were called to the house on more than one occasion. That was a bad time, but it was in the past and he wanted to keep it in the past, so it worried him that she was here. Last he heard from her was that she had remarried and was expecting a child. The big question was what was she doing here now?

Rich could think of nothing else. The next day the same woman came back to the hospital looking for Dr. Sampson. This time Rich was in the emergency room. He was paged to the front desk, and he came out from the exam room and went to the front desk. The woman turned and faced Rich, and Rich said coldly, "Emily, what are you doing here?"

"Hello to you also, Rich," Emily said.

Emily noticed that the nurse was staring, so she asked, "Is there someplace private where we can talk?"

"Yeah, come on. My office is upstairs. Follow me."

Rich told the nurse at the desk that if he was needed he would be in his office. She understood.

Once in his office she had to move some stuff to sit down. "Still see that you're no good at keeping house."

"Cut to the chase, E. You were never any good at small talk. What do you want?"

"Richard, I'm in trouble, I've over-extended myself. They're going to take my home, and they already took my car. I know I have no right asking, but I really am in dire need. Please!"

Rich said, "Maybe you should start at the beginning, because last time I heard of you, you had remarried to a lawyer or something and you were expecting a child. Why don't you start from there?"

"Your information was sort of right. I married a financial advisor and, when the stock market crashed, so did he. I was pregnant, but I miscarried during that same period of time. My crashed financial advisor was stealing from me. When I realized it, he had taken most everything, then he just disappeared. Still to this day I haven't heard from him. He's left me up to my eyeballs in debt. I have creditors coming out of the woodwork at me, and I heard you were working at Bay County, so I took a chance that you could look past our differences and help me out."

Rich just sat there and thought about what she had said, then said, "So, E, how much do you need?"

Emily hesitated, then said, "Thirty thousand would let me keep my home."

Rich's eyes got big. He took a deep breath and said, "The only way that I'll agree to this, if this is a one-time situation."

"Yes, most definitely, I won't come around again," said Emily.

Rich reached into his satchel by his desk, pulled his checkbook out, and wrote her the check for thirty thousand. Before he handed it to her, he said, "There's one stipulation. You'll need to wait until Friday to cash it. I'll have enough funds in there by Friday."

Emily's eyes lit up and she said, "Thank you, Richard. I know how hard this was for you, but you saved me. Thanks again."

She got up, kissed Rich on the cheek, and left his office. Rich slowly rubbed his cheek where Emily had kissed him. Rich just hoped that this wouldn't be a re-occurring thing, but if he were a betting man, he would bet that Emily would be back. After she left, he went back down to the ER and fielded questions from the nurse at the ER desk. Rich just told her that it was his x-wife and left it at that.

Rudy Anderson came in that afternoon and found Rich. Rich was impressed with his progress and told him so. Rudy was beaming with pride. "So you're looking really good. How much weight have you lost?"

Rudy, still beaming proudly, said, "Almost fifty pounds."

Rich replied with a large smile of his own, "Wow! That's great!"

"Dr. Z told me that I'm doing good, but cautioned me not to get ahead of myself. She told me to keep sticking with the program and it'll work. It's been hard but I'm already feeling better and I'm breathing better. Everyday activities are becoming easier and easier."

Rich patted him on the shoulder and replied, "I'm proud of you, Rudy."

Rich could hear the ambulance pulling up in the emergency bay, and Rich told Rudy to come by as often as he wanted, but he needed to go now. Rudy understood, and Rich headed toward the ambulance. Rich and Steve met the ambulance at the door and waited for the EMT's to bring out the patients. There were two ambulances that pulled up almost together. Steve took the first, and Rich waited for the second.

Steve's patient was an unidentified white female who wasn't wearing her seatbelt when involved in a serious motor vehicle accident. She had extreme facial fractures and deep lacerations. Steve did all that he could, but her injuries were too extensive and she died.

The other patient whom Rich had taken was a forty-five-year-old man who was clearly under the influence of alcohol. The man had his seatbelt on and only received minor injuries. Rich looked for some identification and found a driver's license. He gave it to the cop who came into the ER with the accident. He took his name, then ran it through his PDA. He was a repeat offender. He had a DUI on record and was driving with a suspended license. Steve came into the room where Rich was stitching up the sleeping drunk. "I need a second signature of time of death since the female patient is a Jane Doe. She was on the receiving end of your drunk's car."

Rich looked up from stitching the drunk's head and said, "Leave it with the body. I'll go over there; I'm almost finished with this guy."

Steve nodded and Rich finished up. After he was finished with the drunk, he told the nurse to start a banana bag and tell the police officer that he'd be ready to go with him in about forty-five minutes to an hour. The nurse understood and started the man's IV.

Rich went across to the treatment room, grabbed the file, and started to sign the paperwork when something on the body caught his eye. He went over to the body and examined it more closely. Rich's gut was telling him that this was Emily. He needed to find out. He went to find Steve and said, "Can I see you for a second?"

Steve turned toward him and asked, "What's up?"

Rich said as the color drained out of his face, "Steve, I think the Jane Doe who was brought in is my x-wife."

Steve who was shocked by what Rich said, asked, "What makes you think that? This woman has severe facial fractures that make any visual recognition almost impossible."

Rich said, "Yes, I know, but Emily had a birthmark on her right hip that looked like a clown's face. Can you come in and help me roll her?"

Steve and Rich entered the room where the woman's body was still on the exam table. Steve helped Rich roll the woman so that her right hip was exposed. Sure enough, the birthmark looked kind of like a clown's face. Both men were surprised. They rolled her back and pulled the sheet back over her body. Steve asked sadly, "Were you two close?"

"No, I saw her for the first time earlier today; I haven't seen or heard from her in years. Our divorce was messy. She came in today to borrow money and, as usual, I caved in and gave her the money. My last thoughts of her weren't good in nature. I feel bad that my last thoughts of her were bad."

Steve said, "You had no way of knowing that this was going to happen."

Rich nodded and understood what he was saying. Steve patted him on the shoulder and left Rich to be alone with his dead ex-wife. Rich stayed only for a few minutes, then made corrections to the chart and changed the name to Emily Sampson. He wasn't sure if she went back to his name or to her maiden name, which was Crosby, so he decided to put down both and make sure the coroner knew what he was trying to do. Then he was disturbed by a lot a loud noise in the hallway.

Rich came out of the room and right in the middle of what looked like some sort of hostage takeover. A patient had a nurse in front of him and a scalpel to her throat. Rich recognized him as Mr. Peterson, his drug-seeking patient who took him by surprise and beat him up.

They didn't see him, so he went quickly back into the room and called security. They in turn called the local police. Then he went back into the hallway, and Mr. Peterson and his hostage were already down by the elevators.

Steve almost ran right into them and immediately started to try and talk Mr. Peterson away from the nurse whom he was holding hostage. All three went into the stairwell and came out on the mezzanine floor, which housed offices and out-patient admissions. Steve continued to talk to Mr. Peterson. Rich was in the stairwell following them from a distance. Rich heard security coming up the stairs, and Rich stopped them and filled them in on the situation.

Security in turn kept their distance. Once they got to the mezzanine floor, they surrounded Mr. Peterson and that made him even more nervous and jittery. Steve pleaded with security to back off, Mr. Peterson's hand kept getting close to the nurse's throat, and in fact she had a couple of nicks and had blood on her neck that was running onto her scrub top. Steve kept motioning with his eyes first down, then back up at the nurse. Finally she looked at Steve and mouthed that she understood what to do. Steve nodded slightly so as not to draw attention to himself. Security backed off, and Steve could see Mr. Peterson relax just a bit. Steve said, "Mr. Peterson, why don't you let this nurse go and I'll personally take you to a treatment room and give you an injection of your choice. Just let her go. She can't help you get the drugs you need; only I can do that."

Steve watched Mr. Peterson's muscles relax even more and Steve said quickly, "Now!"

The nurse went limp and quickly fell to the floor. Mr. Peterson lost his grip on her, then Steve rushed him, and Steve's momentum carried him and Mr. Peterson up and over the railing. They both fell the single story to the entrance foyer below. For a moment all looked in horror and everything fell silent. Rich ran to the railing and yelled, "Need a crash cart and gurneys to the entrance foyer stat!"

Rich flew down the stairs, ran to the foyer, and went to Steve and Mr. Peterson. Dave came into the foyer immediately after Rich. Rich felt for a pulse on Mr. Peterson and there wasn't one. He was dead. Rich rolled him over onto his back and found that the scalpel had wound up in his chest. Dave went to Steve and felt for a pulse. He had a strong and steady pulse.

Dave called for a c-collar and a backboard so they could get Steve off the floor and into a trauma room to assess his injuries. Once they got him on the backboard, he came to and struggled to breathe. Quickly Rich started some oxygen, which helped. Dave and Rich put Steve on the gurney and wheeled him quickly to trauma room one. There were several nurses and doctors buzzing around Steve. Dave continued to bark orders, "Need a full head and neck and also a chest series. Start an IV."

The radiologist shot the x-rays and quickly they were back. Rich put the x-rays on the light board, and both doctors looked at the films. Both doctors said at the same time, "Fractures of the left clavicle, left second and third, and fourth ribs."

They also took pictures of his left wrist and hand. It was broken badly. Dave called the wrist and hand orthopedist, Dr. Winegarner. He came quickly down to the trauma room and looked at the x-rays.

Dr. Winegarner asked Dave, "What are his other injuries?"

"He has some broken ribs and his clavicle is broken, but his head and neck are clear," said Dave.

"I need to operate on Steve's wrist and hand as soon as possible; he has some severe fractures," said Dr. Winegarner.

Dave asked, "Okay, can you give me about ten to fifteen minutes? I need to tape his ribs, and what about pain medication?"

Dr. Winegarner said, "If you could hold off on the medication, which would make it easier on the anesthesiologist and on Steve."

Dave asked, "How severe are his fractures, Dr. Winegarner?"

Dr. Winegarner looked serious and replied, "Very serious. They could be career ending, but I'll not know until I can get him to surgery."

Both Dave and Rich were surprised by Dr. Winegarner's statements.

Dr. Winegarner said, "My guess is that he fell on his left side and tried to catch himself with his left hand. It's instinct to put a hand out when you fall. In this case, the fall was too high, and the weight behind the fall was too great."

Dave continued to wrap Steve's ribs, then gave Steve to Dr. Winegarner, who had already made his team available and an operating room as well. As soon as Steve was wheeled out of the trauma room, Dave asked, "Can I see you for a moment, Dr. Sampson?"

Rich stayed behind, and everybody left the room except for the two of them. Dave was trying to control his temper and asked, "So, Rich, how did all of this happen? How did Steve wind up falling off the mezzanine?"

"The patient who surprised me and beat me, who was drug seeking, came back. He held a nurse captive with a scalpel to her throat and was demanding drugs. Steve got in the mix, and I called security. Steve was doing a good job talking him down, and finally the nurse slipped away from him. Steve went to go grab him, and their momentum carried both men up and over the railing and onto the entrance foyer floor. I tried to reach out and grab them, but they were moving too fast, and they would have taken me over along with them," said Rich.

Dave just shook his head and said, "This is one situation where Steve should have looked before he leaped."

Rich didn't say anything. Dave said to him, "Sorry, Rich, I'm not blaming you for this. I'm just concerned about Steve. Can you hold down the fort in the ER? I'm going up and wait for him to come out of surgery. I'll send Titus down to help you."

Rich nodded that he would do that, and Dave left to go up to surgery. Dr. Winegarner started surgery almost immediately, and it took almost five hours. There was a lot to repair, and many of Steve's small bones in his wrist and hand were broken so severely that rods, pins, and screws were used to hold the bones in place or in some cases take the place of the bone itself. His hand was a real mess.

Dr. Winegarner also had a vascular surgeon there just to make sure that all Steve's nerves were intact and not affected by all the bone breaks. The vascular surgeon only found one nerve blocked by a broken bone, and that was in the wrist. The surgeon repaired the nerve. Everything else was intact. After the surgery was finished Dr. Winegarner put Steve in a heavy brace, but no cast. When he got to the room he was put in a suspension sling. The sling would increase blood flow and flexibility.

He had many, many stitches in his wrist, hand, and fingers. Steve was looking at the first ten days just resting and no movement, then the stitches would come out and he would then be in a hard cast for four to six weeks, then during that time he would start physical therapy. Dr. Winegarner visited with Dave and shared what he did in surgery. Dave understood, then Dr. Winegarner was paged back into recovery. "Is that Steve?"

Dr. Winegarner nodded, and both doctors went back into the recovery area. A nurse was standing by Steve's bedside holding a basin and watching him throw up. He was in agony as he threw up due to his several broken rib and the pain in his left hand. Dave reminded Dr. Winegarner about his past drug history and made a note of that in his chart. He wrote to limit narcotics, use synthetic medication whenever possible. Dr. Winegarner said to Dave, "I'm going to pass care to you, and I'll be in charge of the care of his hand only."

Dave agreed and told the nurse to add ten ccs of Darvocet and Compazine for the pain and nausea to his list of drugs. The nurse added the drugs and immediately Steve started to calm down.

For the next couple of days Dave gave Steve as much synthetic drugs as possible, but he needed the good stuff because, between his ribs and his hand, he was in constant pain.

After the third day his rib pain started to subside somewhat, and he was immediately taken off the narcotics and given Tylenol three and anti-inflammatory medications. Dave came into his room on the afternoon of the third day, and Steve was alert and talkative. "That was a stupid stunt. You could have killed yourself."

Steve replied slowly, "At the time and moment, I had to make a judgment call, and the nurse already had cuts to her throat. I wasn't going to watch while that drug addict sliced up one of my nurses. He started to relax somewhat when the officers backed away, and I motioned to the nurse to fall to the floor and, when she did, I ran at him and we went up and over the balcony. I wasn't planning for both of us to go over. I was hoping just Mr. Peterson would go over. Did he survive?"

Dave said, "No, the scalpel lodged in his chest during the fall."

"I'm sorry for that, but my only goal was to save my nurse," replied Steve.

Dave asked, "I understand; how is your pain level today?"

"My ribs aren't as painful today, and my wrist and hand aren't too bad."

Dave checked the color of Steve's fingers. His color was good, and all were warm and pink. "Can you move your fingers?"

Steve could move all fingers except his pinky and ring finger. "So what type of damage did I do to myself?"

"You broke your left clavicle and a few ribs on that side and your hand and wrist were badly broken. Dr. Winegarner took five hours to put your hand back together. He should be in sometime today to explain all of that and your recovery plan," replied Dave.

"I'm going to be able to use my hand again, right?"

"Dr. Winegarner didn't mention that you wouldn't have the use of your hand. All the nerves were okay and intact. It was mainly bone and muscles that were repaired. Let him explain that to you."

Steve was still worried, but more at ease. Dr. Winegarner came in, sat next to his bedside, and told him about his injuries and what he did surgically to fix the problem. Steve was surprised that there was so much damage done. Dr. Winegarner pulled out a needle attached to a syringe that had medication already in it. "What are you doing?"

"I'm going to give you a local so I can un-bandage you and clean, then redress your hand," said Dr. Winegarner.

"Sorry about jumping on you like that, but I have to be careful," replied Steve.

"I understand. Dave filled me in. This is going to burn, so be prepared," said Dr. Winegarner.

Steve prepared himself, and Dr. Winegarner injected the medication just below the wrist area. He then waited a few minutes and injected more of the medication into his thumb. That was painful. Dave was watching from the other side of the bed. After the medication was injected, he got all of his supplies and equipment ready. He was slow and methodical. He looked at his watch and said, "Okay, Steve, I'm going to cut the bandages off. Now remember that there will be a lot of stitches and swelling. If any of this hurts at any time, please let me know immediately."

Steve nodded, and Dr. Winegarner continued to cut the bandages off and expose his hand. Everybody in the room couldn't believe how bad his hand looked. Slowly and carefully Dr. Winegarner cleaned and examined all aspects of his fingers, thumb, hand, and wrist. Dr. Winegarner was happy with the way his hand looked. He was concerned about the pinky and ring finger and wasn't sure why Steve couldn't move them. He studied the fingers and wanted an x-ray to double check his work. After the x-ray came back Steve asked, "Is everything okay?"

Dr. Winegarner replied, "Just wanted to double check your pinky and ring finger. Not sure why you can't move them at this point. Are they painful?"

"No, not really; more of a heavy feeling and a stiff feeling than pain," explained Steve.

"Then mobility should come back. The x-rays looked good. Please be patient. This will be a process. I'm going to bandage your hand, and we'll do this again in another couple of days. In the meantime keep typing to move those fingers. I also want you on antibiotics while you're in the hospital. I don't want a hospital-born infection to ruin all my good work."

Steve thanked him and Dr. Winegarner left Steve's room. Steve looked at Dave and said, "How much longer do you anticipate me being a patient?"

"Not sure yet, depends on Dr. Winegarner, but nobody is in a hurry except for you, so settle down and get used to being a patient."

All laughed, and Rich got paged to the ER. Steve said, "Take good care of my department."

"No problem," replied Rich.

Dave left as well, because the local that was given to Steve was starting to affect him, and he was asleep before Dave left the room. Steve slept till late that evening. His hand, head, and ribs were all throbbing. He pressed the nurse call button, and a nurse quickly came to his room. "Can I get some pain medication?"

The nurse looked at his chart and said, "Yes, Dr. Pratt, I'll be right back."

The nurse left his room and went to the drug cart, typed in the information, and the cart automatically dispensed the medication. The nurse came back into Steve's room with the medication, poured some water, and she gave the pills and the water to Steve. He took the pills. While the nurse was there she took a set of vital signs and realized that his blood pressure was elevated and also his temperature was up just a little. It was 99. 3 and his BP was 190 over 87. The nurse noted that in his chart and was concerned enough to pick up the phone and call Dr. Bradfield.

Luckily, Dave was still in his office when the nurse called. Dave told her that he'd be right down. Dave stopped the paperwork that he was working on and went to Steve's room. The night nurse who called Dave was there and had a new set of vitals. This set was almost the same, only his temperature was even more elevated than before; it was 100. 7. The antibiotics were up and running. Steve was breathing shallow. Dave didn't like how things were going. He tried to wake Steve up, but he couldn't.

He called Dr. Winegarner and got his service, so Dave left a message, then he took things into his own hands. Dave called the intensive care unit and said that he was bringing a patient and needed a bed. The ICU told Dave that it would be no problem to go ahead and bring the patient up. Dave and the nurse moved Steve to the ICU, and Dave stayed with him the rest of the night. Despite the antibiotics running wide open, Steve's fever went up and down most of the night. Dave also increased his oxygen level and it seemed to help. His breathing wasn't so shallow.

The rest of the night Dave dozed in the chair next to Steve's bed, and Steve was restless, but unconscious. Steve finally started to come around the next morning. Steve was coughing as he awoke, and it hurt his ribs to do so. That woke up Dave, and he stood, looked at Steve, and said, "When did you start to cough?"

Steve replied, "I woke up with it. Just a dry cough; don't worry so much, Dave."

Dave left the ICU and told the nurses to keep an eye out on Steve and his cough. By lunch the dry, non-productive cough had become a full blown, mucus producing cough, followed by blood. The nurse had seen enough and called Dave. Dave told her to take Steve to radiology and he wanted a chest x-ray, then he also wanted an MRI. The x-ray showed the broken rib, but he couldn't tell if the lung was injured until he looked at the MRI. Sure enough, when Dave looked at the MRI he found a small tear in the side of his lung. Rich was paged, and Steve went directly to the operating room. Rich studied the MRI and could fix the tear with laparoscopic surgery. He would have to give Steve narcotics for the procedure, so after the procedure Steve became violently ill. Dave guessed that was how the tear happened in the first place.

Steve was held down while he threw up, so as not to complicate anything that was just done. He was given Compazine, which slowed his vomiting, then with another dose stopped it. The Compazine had its side effects as well. It caused him to have extreme dry mouth and a headache, and that ended up being a monster.

After the vomiting had stopped, Steve was moved back to the ICU, just a precaution. Between the medication and the surgery, he would most likely sleep for the rest of the late afternoon and into the evening. Dave was running on empty as well, and Rich said to him, "Dave, Steve is going to sleep for the rest of the evening and most of the night, and you should as well."

Dave replied, "You're right, but I don't feel like I can go home. If you need me or Steve would need me, I'll be in my office."

"Okay, but please try and get some sleep. You look like an ad for dead. I say that because I care." And Rich laughed.

Dave smirked and thanked him sarcastically, then went upstairs to his office. He lay on the couch and in no time was asleep. Dave slept hard until his secretary came in and as quietly as she could was searching for something on his desk. Without moving or without even opening his eyes, Dave asked, "Rose, what are you looking for?"

This startled Rose, and she nearly jumped out of her skin. After Rose caught her breath, she whispered, "I need the inventory sheets for last month. They're due today."

"Stand behind my desk. Now, the file should be on your right about three or four file folders down. I did finish it, and it's signed," said Dave.

Rose shuffled through some file folders and found it just about where he said it would be. With the file in hand she said as she was leaving, "Sorry to disturb you."

Dave asked, "What time is it?"

"Almost nine," Rose said softly.

Rose left, and Dave laid there and rested, but didn't go back to sleep. Dave finally got up, showered, put a fresh pair of scrubs on, and went down to the ICU to check on Steve. Rich was curled up sleeping in the chair next to Steve's bed. Steve was awake, but still had the breathing tube from the procedure yesterday.

Dave came up to his bedside put a hand on his shoulder and whispered, "You had a nick on your lung and Rich repaired it with laparoscopic surgery. Rich wanted to make sure your airway wasn't compromised."

Rich uncoiled himself, yawned, stood, looked at Steve, then at his oxygen saturation level. He was at 100%.

Rich said, "I'm going to take the tube out now. You know the drill. When I pull the tube out, you cough."

Rich turned the machine off, then unhooked the tape and deflated the tube, then he counted to three and Rich pulled the tube out as Steve coughed. Rich put him on oxygen just to help him recover from the tube being pulled. Dave gave him a few ice chips to soothe his raw throat.

"Thank you both for saving my life," Steve said in a whisper.

Dave said, "You need to rest and recover; you've been through a lot."

Steve closed his eyes and slept.

The next couple of days Steve was improving and no further complications occurred. He was moved out of the intensive care unit and back to a regular room. Dr. Winegarner came in and said, "Steve, I heard you had a rough couple of days."

Steve, who was still somewhat hoarse from the tube, said, "Yeah, I can move my pinky. I still can't move my ring finger."

"Okay, I'm going to give you the local, and we're going to un-bandage, clean, and x-ray the hand and wrist," said Dr. Winegarner.

Dr. Winegarner loaded the syringe and injected the medication, then waited and injected his thumb. Then he waited, and lined up all his equipment and started slowly and methodically cutting off the bandages. Then he washed the area and checked all the stitches. Everything looked good. The swelling and the bruising had started to subside.

He manipulated both his pinky finger and ring finger and said, "Everything looks good, Steve. You're healing nicely. I just want another x-ray, then I'll re-bandage you and put a heavy splint on. The next time I see you, I'll remove the stitches and apply a hard cast to your fingers, hand, and wrist."

Steve asked, "How long will I be in the hard cast?"

"Six to eight weeks. Then after the hard cast comes off, it'll be another hard splint and lots of physical therapy. This will be a slow process, and you're going to have to be patient enough to see it through or there's an outside chance that you may not get full use of your hand back," replied Dr. Winegarner.

Steve looked sullen and replied, "Dr. Winegarner, I'll do whatever it takes to get my full mobility back. Whether you realize it or not, being a doctor here at Bay County is the most important thing in my life, I won't jeopardize that."

"I know," replied Dr. Winegarner.

The x-rays came back, and they all looked good. So Dr. Winegarner bandaged his finger, hand, and wrist and put on the hard splint that he'd been wearing. Steve was getting sleepy from the local and didn't even manage to stay awake until Dr. Winegarner was finished. Dr. Winegarner said to Dave, "In all my years of practicing, I've never seen an adult react that way to the local that I give to post-op patients."

"He's been like that since I've known him. Remember to use as much synthetic medication as possible," said Dave.

Dr. Winegarner nodded in understanding.

The next couple of weeks passed slowly, and Steve was now being impatient and wanted out of the hospital. Dr. Winegarner came in, took out the stitches, applied the hard cast, then said, "Now that I've got you in the hard cast, I'm releasing you. It's up to Dave to release you medically."

Dave was there and Steve asked, "So what about it, Dave? When can I get out of here?"

Dave replied, "Is this afternoon soon enough for you?"

"Now you're talking."

All of Steve's IV's had been disconnected a couple of days ago, so he was ready to go. Dave wrote the couple of scripts that he would need and said to him, "I'll get you a set of scrubs. Your clothes were cut off when you came into the trauma room."

Steve said, "I had only worn that shirt twice, and the jeans cost me almost eighty bucks. Man, what a rip off."

Dave replied laughingly, "What a diva!"

Steve laughed with Dave. Dave wrote him the scripts, and he was on his way. Steve got dressed, then took the scripts from Dave. Steve asked, "I never asked anybody; can I drive?"

"I guess so. Is your car here?"

"Yeah, it's in the parking lot."

Dave thought for a moment, then said, "Okay, but you need to be careful with your hand. When is your first physical therapy session?"

"I'll be careful, mother. My first physical therapy session is tomorrow, next door at the Glassman Clinic. The physical therapist is Monica Anderson. I haven't met her, but she sounds promising."

Dave smiled, shook his head, and said, "Remember why you are going to physical therapy; not to date Monica, but to make sure you have full mobility in your hand and wrist."

Steve rolled his eyes and said, "Yes, yes, I know."

Both Dave and Steve walked out together, and Steve went home and crashed. The next morning Steve showed up for his first physical therapy session. Dr. Winegarner wasn't kidding; it was painful and intense. On his way home he got all of his scripts filled, went home, and immediately took a pain pill. That helped a lot.

The next couple of weeks were painful and physically demanding. His hand and wrist throbbed after every session. Then Steve's cast came off, and the physical therapy sessions were even more painful and more physically demanding on his hand, wrists and fingers. Finally after the twelfth week he had all of his mobility back and was released by Monica to go back to work. He needed to wear a soft brace specifically made for him by Monica.

As Steve came back to work he found that his grip was not yet as strong as he wanted it to be, so he called Monica, and she gave Steve some extra strengthening exercises. Soon that increased and his grip strength was almost back to normal.

Steve had settled back into the ER, and once again Bay County was back to the status quo. But unfortunately the status quo does not stay status very long at Bay County Hospital.

CHAPTER 9

Steve had to do his ride along shift with the paramedics for his recertification that's due at the end of the month, and he had only two more days to get it done. He wasn't procrastinating; he just plain forgot. The ER had been short a doctor for several months due to an illness. Steve finally got a replacement for his shift and took the seven to seven shift on truck 8, which was based out of Bay County. Tom and Jason were the paramedics on truck 8; they were both experienced, good men. Steve picked up the ambulance at the emergency entrance when they brought their first patient in.

Both Tom and Jason knew Steve well. They knew that he wasn't always by the book, but he was the best ER doctor that they had ever seen work. Tom and Jason were both glad to see him for his ride along recertification.

The shift started off quiet, then by mid-day they ran several calls in a row. The first was a heart-related call; the patient was already dead before they arrived. The next call was that of a domestic disturbance. When the ambulance arrived on scene, which was a home in a decent neighborhood, the officer at the scene greeted the ambulance and told Tom, who was driving, that it was not yet safe for them to enter the scene. Steve, who was riding in the back and was looking out the back window, yelled to the front, "There are people shot in that front yard!"

The officer spoke up to be heard by Steve, "Dr. Pratt, I know they're lying on the front yard, but we need to secure the shooter, who's still in the house. We're waiting for SWAT, which is on their way, and its protocol."

Both Tom and Jason understood this, but Steve thought it was wrong, so all he could do for now was to look out the back of the ambulance and watch the bodies on the front lawn. Then he saw two of the three bodies move. Steve about jumped out of his skin. He grabbed the medic bag and yelled at Tom and Jason as he was going out the back doors of the ambulance, "They're moving, guys, I'm not going to wait until they stop!"

Quickly Steve was outside the ambulance ducking behind cars and bushes. Both Tom and Jason yelled at him, and the officer was also yelling at him. Tom and Jason both grabbed their medic bags, shook their heads at each other, and followed Steve outside.

When the shooter in the house saw movement he started shooting again. All three immediately dove for cover. From the sound of the gunfire and how rapid it was, all guessed the shooter had some type of automatic weapon, maybe even more than one.

Steve was just a few feet away from one of the victims. Steve was behind a parked car and yelled at the victim, and that person moved slightly. Steve continued to talk with the victim using hand signals, mainly thumbs up and down, depending on what Steve was asking.

The shooting stopped, and Steve made his move to grab the victim whom he'd been communicating with. Both Tom and Jason saw what Steve was getting ready to do. They both tried to draw the fire of the shooter. At first it was working, then the shooter switched his line of fire from Tom and Jason to Steve. Steve had grabbed the victim and had started dragging him to safety when Steve took a bullet in the shoulder. He staggered, but continued to drag the victim to safety. He finally managed to get the victim to safety behind a parked car. Immediately Steve started to treat the patient. Tom and Jason quickly moved to Steve.

SWAT arrived and quickly took over the scene. The shooter focused on the SWAT team. Steve quickly ran out from behind the car to grab another victim, even though Steve was bleeding from his shoulder and blood was running down his right arm and dripping off of his right hand. Steve got to the second victim and was dragging the victim toward

Fiction - Mystery

LADY ACE
SANDRA FARRIS

Kasey O'Brien's life has always been about airplanes; what makes them tick, what makes them fly. When her father's plane crashes into a Colorado mountainside, she takes over their failing air charter service and is determined to make it work.

On a charter flight with a passenger on board to Oregon's Briar Meadows Ranch, the left engine of Cimmaron Air's Beech Baron freezes up on final approach. Kasey O'Brien has to set the plane down at the ranch without the aide of emergency services, thus earning her the nickname, Lady Ace.

During inspection of the engine, she discovers an oil line has been purposely c and is forced to stay there until a replacement can be flown in. While at t ranch, she is captivated by the earthy and entirely masculine foreman, Cc Navarro. But Kasey has to conquer the intrigue that surrounds Cort as we What is he hiding? And what is next for Kasey? Since he had failed, would tl saboteur make another attempt on her life—or was her passenger his target?

www.sandrafarris.com

$15.95

ISBN 978-1-4401-1967-5

90000

9 781440 119675

safety when the shooter turned his fire on Steve. Steve went down in a heap.

Both Tom and Jason ducked low behind the car as glass flew along the tops of their heads. That's when the SWAT team rushed the house. They shot tear gas and busted the front door down, and in a blaze of gunfire the SWAT team entered the house and shot the gunman. As soon as the SWAT team leader yelled that the scene was clear, both Tom and Jason went into the yard and started to treat the injured. One of the shooting victims on the yard was dead, but the other two were alive.

Two more ambulances showed up on scene, went into the yard, and helped the injured. With the extra help, Tom and Jason could now focus their attention on Steve. Steve's injuries included the bullet wound just below the right clavicle and the other bullet wound just above his belt-line to the right of the midline. A third bullet had grazed his right forehead just above his eyebrow. Tom and Jason started an IV, packed his wounds, immobilized him on a spine board, and transported him to Bay County.

Steve was still mostly conscious as they were loading him into the ambulance and he said to Tom and Jason, "You know, fellows, I don't think I'm that bad. My shoulder is talking to me, but other than that I don't have much pain."

Both Tom and Jason looked at each other and quickly loaded him into the ambulance and drove quickly to Bay County. Once at the emergency entrance Tom and Jason unloaded him, and Dave and Titus were there to take Steve to trauma room 3. Tom took Dave aside and said, "Dr. Bradfield, Dr. Pratt was mostly conscious in the field and told Jason and me that his shoulder was hurting, but nothing else really hurt, which as you know could mean signs of paralysis."

Dave thanked him and quickly went back to Steve and shared the information he learned from Tom with the rest of the trauma team. Titus tested his lower extremities; Steve had some movement, but not much feeling. Dave and Titus quickly packed his wounds and took him to get a CT scan. Dave and Titus wanted to know where the bullet was and what damage it had done.

They loaded him into the scanner, went into the viewing room, and watched the monitor as Steve was being scanned. The bullet in his shoulder was lodged in the soft muscle tissue and would be easy to extract, as the scan continued, it revealed the location of the next bullet. To everybody's fear, the bullet was right up next to Steve's lower vertebra. From what they could make out from the scan, the vertebra looked crushed from the impact of the bullet. The bullet could have pushed some bone fragments into Steve's spinal cord and that could account for Steve's lack of feeling. As soon as the scan was finished, Dave asked Titus, "Can you do this surgery?"

Titus replied, "I'd rather not; my specialty isn't the back. Dr. Owens is on staff, and he specializes in the back and spine. I've never worked with him."

Titus's recommendation was enough for him. Dave called Dr. Owens, and he came down and looked at the scans and x-rays. Dr. Owens studied the scans and the x-rays, and to Dave he seemed too over-confident, but at that time he didn't say anything. Dr. Owens knew exactly what needed to happen, and he shared the specifics with Dave. Dave was in agreement, but still didn't care for his mannerisms. Dr. Owens scheduled the surgery for first thing in the morning.

Dave went back into Steve's room and shared what Dr. Owens was planning on doing. Suddenly the reality of his condition set in, and Steve knew this was serious. Steve consented to the surgery, and Steve, in somewhat a shaky voice, asked, "Am I going to come out of this being able to walk?"

"As far as Dr. Owens is concerned, there should be no problem. According to him, the bullet hit one of your lower vertebras and pieces from that are lodged near your spinal cord, and that's what's causing your loss of feeling."

Steve nodded in understanding, but was still pretty shaken.

That night Dave stayed with Steve, and Dave asked, "Steve, what were you thinking out in the field today? You could have gotten yourself and others killed."

"Yeah, I know, but, Dave, when I saw those people just lying helplessly in that front yard and the police telling us in the ambulance that the scene wasn't safe and that we would have to wait, I looked out and saw one of the patients moving. Something inside me just snapped and, before I knew it, I had grabbed the medic bag and was outside the ambulance dodging bullets."

Dave said, "Obviously, you didn't dodge the bullets very well."

"You're not kidding!"

Steve was starting to yawn, and his eyelids were getting heavy. "Steve, you need to sleep. You have a big day tomorrow."

Steve closed his eyes and slept on and off for the rest of the night. Before Dave drifted off, he said a little prayer under his breath. All he wanted was for Steve to come out of this okay.

Bright and early the next morning a couple of orderlies and a surgical nurse came into Steve's room and got him prepared for surgery. Shortly after that they wheeled him to the operating room, and Dave was by his side. The last thing Steve mumbled before he was wheeled into the OR was, "Please let me come out of this being able to walk."

Dave patted Steve on the arm and tried to calm his fears the best he could. They wheeled him into the OR. All Dave could do was wait. The first hour seemed to go by rather quickly. It was the next three hours that went on and on. Dave wished that he'd scrubbed in, but didn't think it was appropriate. Dave thought that Dr. Owens might think he was looking over his shoulder, so Dave stayed in the waiting room, which was hard to do.

Finally, Dr. Owens walked out of the OR. Dave tried to read his facial expression. He couldn't. Dave stood, approached Dr. Owens, and asked, "How did it go?"

"Let's sit down," said Dr. Owens.

They both sat down, and Dr. Owens said, "His shoulder was no problem. Removed the bullet, there was no damage to the bone. The graze wound on his forehead took eight stitches. The vertebras affected were actually L4 and L5. The fragments were indeed close to the spinal cord. One of the fragments actually penetrated the cord, but didn't cut it. I repaired both of the vertebra and removed all the fragments, including the fragment that had penetrated the cord. We tested his reflexes in both legs, and they were good. As far as mobility and feeling, we'll have to wait until he's awake and alert."

Dr. Owens's attitude was that of superiority, and Dave could hardly stomach it. Dave thanked him, and Dr. Owens returned to the OR. Dave went to recovery and waited for Steve to come out of the anesthesia. It was another two hours before Steve was awake and alert enough to test his mobility and feeling. Dr. Owens and Dave were both there to help him sit up. Steve was suffering the side effects from all the sedation given to him during the operation. Steve mumbled, "Hey, fellows, not so fast. I'm seeing big black spots in front of my eyes."

Steve closed his eyes as he sat at the edge of the bed. A nurse grabbed a basin and held it in front of Steve. Steve opened his eyes, then he did throw up. He felt somewhat better after he was finished vomiting. With Dr. Owens on one side and Dave on the other side, they helped him to his feet. "Okay, Steve, you're up. Tell me how you feel?"

Steve caught his breath and replied, "I can feel both of my legs. They feel rubbery, but they're there."

Dr. Owens asked, "Can you take a couple of steps?"

Again with the aid of Dave and Dr. Owens, Steve took a couple of steps. They were more like shuffles, but at that point Dr. Owens was satisfied that all was well. They put Steve back into bed and let him get comfortable, and he quickly fell asleep. Steve slept another three or four hours. Dave wasn't in Steve's room when he woke up; a nurse was in his room taking a set of vitals.

Steve woke up suddenly and was in severe pain. The nurse called Dr. Owens and also Dave. Dave and Dr. Owens arrived at the same time. Dr. Owens pulled back his covers and asked Steve as he poked his legs with the end of his pen. He had feeling all the way to about mid-thigh, then there wasn't any feeling. Steve was sweating, and his blood pressure was way up. "Where is most of your pain, Steve?"

Steve, in short bursts, replied, "From my knee up to my hips and into my lower back. The pain is severe."

Dr. Owens told Dave to go ahead and give Steve something for the pain and that he needed an MRI and CT scan of his lower back and legs. Dave injected pain medication directly into his IV and opened the flow meter wide open. Steve quickly started to get the drug, and slowly the pain subsided enough to move him to radiology to get the MRI and the CT. But as quickly as the pain went, the pain came back with a vengeance when Steve was having his MRI.

He knew that he had to be still, so he tried hard to lie there quietly. He couldn't take the severity of the pain any longer. Steve started to moan, and the technician pressed the intercom and said, "Dr. Pratt, I'm almost done. Hang in there just a while longer."

"It hurts so much, I'm not sure that I can."

The technician stopped the MRI, got him out of the machine, and quickly brought in Dave. Dave rushed to him, and Steve's face was flushed, and he was crying. Steve grabbed onto Dave and said, "I can't handle this, Dave. The pain is so intense. Please help me." He sobbed.

"I gave you enough pain medication to get you through both your scans. I'm calling Dr. Owens. Something needs to be done; he had to have missed something," said Dave.

Dave gave Steve more pain medication, which only took the edge off. His breathing had become depressed, so Dave hesitated to give him much more than he did. Dr. Owens came in and went over the results from the CT scan and MRI and said, "Why were these scans not completed?"

But what was on the scans surprised both doctors. There was a lone fragment of bone inter-twined in a large nerve close to the site of L4 and L5. Dr. Owens pointed it out and said, "As soon as there's an opening in the OR schedule, we'll take him back to surgery and fish out that fragment."

Dave said, trying not to lose his temper, "First, Steve was in too much pain to continue through the scans. That's why they weren't finished. Dr. Owens, how much time do you need to get your team together and scrub?"

Dr. Owens looked taken back and replied, "I'm not sure how much time, maybe thirty minutes."

Dave said, using all the restraint not to beat the crap out of him, "Then I suggest you get ready. I'll meet you in operating room one in twenty minutes."

Dr. Owens stormed out, and Dave and the orderly pushed Steve toward the operating room. Dave grabbed Titus on the way to the OR and said, "If it's the last thing I do, I want Dr. Owens out of this hospital. If I didn't need him to operate on Steve, I would have knocked him out. He missed a fragment that's now almost completely imbedded in a large nerve near his L4 and L5. I'm scrubbing in and this time watching every move he makes."

"Okay, calm down. Let's just get Steve through this first, then you can start the process of firing Dr. Owens," said Titus.

Dave and Dr. Owens got scrubbed and the operation began. Dr. Owens retrieved the fragment and repaired the nerve. He closed the incision, dressed the wound, and sent Steve to post-op.

As soon as Dave could get Steve conscious, he checked him out, and he had all the feeling and most of the mobility back in both legs. Dave was relieved. Dave sought out Dr. Owens and told him that he wanted him off Bay County property immediately. "Is this because I missed the fragment?"

"That is part of it, and your ego is just too big to be in this hospital," replied Dave.

Dr. Owens didn't say anything; he just left. After Steve was out of post-op, he was moved to a room on the third floor, where rehab and physical therapy was housed. As soon as Steve was awake, physical therapy was waiting for him to get started. They were aggressive with him and got him on his feet quickly. Steve responded well and rebounded nicely.

The physical therapist released him after two weeks, then the next week released him back to part-time duty with the aid of a cane, which promptly he lost his first day back. Dave came looking for Steve and found him with a patient. Steve saw Dave stick his head in and nodded that he'd be out in a moment. Dave closed the door quietly and waited outside the treatment room, when Steve finally came out limping slightly. "What did you do to the cane that you're supposed to be using? Aren't you only supposed to be working half-days?"

"Guilty as charged. Yes, I'm only supposed to be working half days, but you know how it is down here. Most days it's almost impossible to get away and, in my own defense, I had my cane and laid it aside. When I came back, it wasn't there," said Steve.

Dave shook his head and said as he walked away, "Steve, you'll never change, and I hope you never do."

Steve chuckled at Dave's comment, and Dave left and Steve went back into the treatment room. He continued to work a full shift.

CHAPTER 10

The emergency room was particularly busy because it was starting to get warmer, and many people were outside doing chores or maintenance on their homes and property after a long, hard winter. Some of the injuries that Steve and his department were seeing were broken bones, cuts, bruises, and even a few eye injuries.

Steve had casted, stitched, and put ice on many patients' injuries. Some of the ways patients managed to hurt themselves was almost comical, but by afternoon Steve was too tired to do any laughing.

Steve came out of a treatment room after stitching up yet another patient. The nurse finished dressing the patient's wound, and Steve wrote a script for an antibiotic and a script for some pain medication and gave those scripts to the nurse. He told the nurse to give the scripts to the patient, then release her. The nurse did as he asked. Steve went to the nurse's desk and grabbed yet another chart. Steve looked at the name on the chart and called from the waiting room the name on the top of the chart. A young boy stood and was assisted by his parents. Once in the exam room Steve said, "Okay, Mr. Rick Simmons, what did you do to your arm?"

Ricky looked quickly at his father, then to his mother, and answered, "I was climbing the tree in my back yard and I fell."

Steve smiled at him, then moved closer to him and said, "Okay, let's take a look at that arm."

Steve reached for Ricky's arm and he flinched. Steve, in the most calming voice, said, "I just need to look at your arm. I'll do my best not to hurt you."

Ricky gave his arm to Steve. Steve gently took his arm and examined it. There was a specific deformity in the middle of his forearm. Steve was looking for scratches and other bruising, because just the broken arm wasn't consistent with a fall from a tree. Steve didn't find any such things, and that sent red flags up. "Okay, young man, we're going to get an x-ray of that arm, just to make sure it's broken, but my guess is that it is."

Ricky asked, "Is that going to hurt?"

"No, the x-ray technician has taken many pictures of broken arms. He'll take good care of your arm."

Mr. Simmons asked, "Dr. Pratt, can I go with Ricky to x-ray?"

Steve replied, "There isn't a need, and besides, you can't go in while they're taking the x-ray."

Mr. Simmons insisted.

Steve replied, "I need you to stay here and fill-out the paperwork. He won't be long."

The x-ray technician came and put him into a wheelchair and rolled him down to radiology. Steve stepped out of the room and quickly went to the computer and typed Ricky's name in. Soon it came up with Ricky's past history. He printed the page out and quickly looked at it, and his thoughts went quickly to abuse. This was the boy's sixth visit to an ER or immediate care facility.

Steve went back into the exam room where Mr. Simmons' was pacing back and forth, and Mrs. Simmons sat in a chair, but was fidgeting. Steve said upon entering the room, "Mr. Simmons, please sit down. I'd like to ask you both a few questions about Ricky's health."

Both parents looked uneasy and upset. Mr. Simmons said, "Why? What's wrong? I just thought Ricky had a broken arm?"

Steve, in a non-threatening voice, replied, "Yes, he does but if he indeed did fall out of a tree, his injuries are somewhat inconsistent. He should have other scratches or bruises. I pulled his past medical records and he's had a lot of visits to the emergency rooms and immediate care facilities in the area."

Mr. Simmons responded aggressively, "I didn't physically see him fall from the tree and, for his other injuries, Ricky is an accident-prone kid."

Steve, who was trying not to get aggressive, asked, "Okay, but how did Ricky break his coccyx or his tailbone? That's not a common clumsy accident."

Mr. Simmons, still defensive, said, "As I remember right, it was when Ricky was learning to ride his bike, and he fell and landed mostly on the cross-bar of his bike."

Steve asked, "Ricky is your only child?"

"That's right," replied Mr. Simmons.

Just then Ricky was wheeled back into the exam room. The technician gave Steve the x-rays, and he put them on the light board and turned it on. Steve looked at the pictures, and it was a greenstick fracture, which again wasn't consistent with the story being told. More and more Steve was leaning toward abuse. Steve turned the light off on the board and said, "Well, your arm is fractured, but it's called a greenstick fracture."

Mr. Simmons asked, "What does that mean?"

Steve replied, "It's when the bone is bent and splits, causing an incomplete fracture. In other words, it's not fracture all the way I'm going to cast it anyway, so that way it'll heal properly. I'll be right back with the cast material. We have blue, green, red; which do you want, Ricky?"

"Blue," said Ricky excited.

Steve left the exam room and quickly called Dave. Steve voiced his suspicions about abuse. Dave told him that he'd be right down. Steve told him where he was and that he was in the process of casting the boy's arm. Steve went back into the exam room with all the cast material. Steve set-up all the materials and started to cast Ricky's arm. Dave knocked on the exam room door, and Steve knew that it was Dave. He said, "Come in."

Dave entered the exam room and looked at Mr. and Mrs. Simmons. Mr. Simmons stood and approached Dave.

"Dr. Bradfield, it's nice to see you again."

Dave at first couldn't place him, then his face came to him and he said, "Stan Simmons, you used to be my financial advisor."

Stan shook hands and asked, "So, Stan, this is little Ricky. Last time I saw him was when he just learned how to crawl."

Ricky smiled, and Steve continued to cast Ricky's arm. "So, Stan, Dr. Pratt is concerned about the number of accidents and injuries Ricky has sustained. Is there any light you could shed on this situation?"

Stan, even though he knew Dave, got defensive and said in loud voice, "No, like I told Dr. Pratt, Ricky is just an accident-prone kid!"

Steve finished with Ricky and gave his dad his discharge papers and instructions on caring for Ricky's cast. After the Simmons were gone, Dave said, "Okay, tell me your suspicions."

Steve said as he threw away what remained of the casting material, "There are a lot of things that just don't add up. He's had a lot of unrelated injuries, but that in itself isn't as suspicious as when I went to examine him. He flinched as I reached for his arm, even after telling him what I was going to do. Then the injury itself was inconsistent with the story given. I managed to see some old scratches and bruises that were in various stages of healing. All my findings put together with his past medical records add up to abuse, unless you can tell me different."

Dave, who was listening to Steve intently, replied, "No, I'm with you. You've seen these cases more than I have, but you know as well as I do proving abuse is difficult."

Steve nodded and said, "That's why when I get some time I want to speak to the doctors who treated Ricky and see if they come up with the same conclusion as I did."

Dave nodded and left the exam room. Steve documented his findings and had some time, so he called around and wanted to talk to others who treated Ricky. All the doctors whom Steve talked to agreed with Steve, but, like Steve, they couldn't prove abuse. One doctor whom Steve talked with even went as far as to call SRS and they looked into the situation. SRS did a home visit and found no immediate threat of harm in the home, and no follow-up was required. Despite all the doctors whom Steve talked to, he knew in his gut that this kid was be physically abused, and nobody had been brave enough to charge the parents.

For the rest of his shift and even after, he carried the thought of Ricky with him. The next day at work Steve did one more thing he could do, then he'd have to let it go because there wasn't enough evidence. He sent an e-mail to all clinics and emergency rooms in the area and made them aware of a possible abuse situation with a patient and gave them the name of Ricky and also sent his medical records with the e-mail.

Ricky's case stayed with Steve for a while. The weeks had passed, and one afternoon when things were slow, Steve was checking his e-mail and opened an e-mail from a doctor at an immediate care clinic who reported seeing Ricky Simmons. The doctor e-mailed Steve that he gave Ricky Simmons three stitches about his left eye. The e-mail also stated that the patient ran into the monkey bars at the park. Steve replied to the e-mail and thanked the doctor for his response. Steve added that injury to the long list of Ricky's so-called accidents. Once again Ricky was on Steve's mind.

Then again weeks passed, and Ricky slipped from Steve's mind. Then one night early in Steve's shift, an ambulance called in and told a nurse who answered the radio call that they were bringing in a young male patient with severe head trauma. The paramedic said into the radio, "Bay County, we're at your emergency entrance."

The nurse ran quickly to find Steve and told him that an ambulance was pulling into the emergency entrance. Steve went out to meet the ambulance. The doors opened and the paramedic pulled out the gurney and, to Steve's surprise, Ricky was lying on the gurney unconscious and had blood and cerebral spinal fluid coming from both ears. He had a large goose-egg size bump on the left side of his forehead, and his face looked like it had been used for a punching bag. Ricky's whole left side of his face and head was red and purple from a fist pounding on his face. His left eye was already swollen shut, and he was even missing teeth.

Steve, outraged, asked the paramedic, "Who did this to the boy?"

The paramedic responded, "When we got to the scene, the police were already there, and they had cuffs on both the wife and the husband. The police were reading them their rights as they took them from the house."

The paramedic took his gurney and left the trauma room. Steve, the nurses and Titus were all working feverishly on Ricky. It was touch and go. Steve needed to intubate, but there was too much blood. He continued to suction, then finally got a clear line of sight and he put the tube past the cords and Ricky was successful intubate. The nurses hooked Ricky up to the ventilator, and his oxygen saturation level started to come up. He stitched and bandaged all that he could. Ricky would need a CT scan and an MRI of his head and neck to see if Ricky would need surgery. They rushed him through both scans; his vitals were shaky at best. The results came back, and it wasn't good news. He had several hematomas. Some looked as if they had calcified, and others were actively bleeding.

Titus looked at Steve, who was still staring at the CT and the MRI, and Titus said, "Steve, this is more than I or you can handle. You should call Dr. Tim O'Connor. He's one of our pediatric neurosurgeons."

Steve called him, and he came quickly and looked at the scans, then looked at Steve and said, "Dr. Pratt, I'm not sure even if I operate, I can save him. There's way too much damage, and even by some small miracle he survives the surgery, he'll surely have permanent brain damage."

Steve looked disappointed and said, dejected, "Then we're supposed to just let this seven-year-old boy die!"

Dr. O'Conner, said, "Okay, I'll try, but I'll make no promises."

Dr. O'Connor took Ricky up to surgery. He opened his skull and started to remove some of the old clots. He cauterized the bleeding of the hematomas. Suddenly blood spurted up from where he was working, and Ricky's monitor started to make all kinds of noise. Dr. O'Connor stopped the bleeding, then told the nurse to get the paddles ready. He set the machine to 100 and defibrillated Ricky. The monitor now was making a continuous beep. He was flat line. Dr. O'Connor exhausted every measure, but it was to no avail. Ricky was dead.

Dr. O'Connor looked up at the clock and told the nurse that the time of death was 6:35 p.m. Dr. O'Connor came out of the OR, and Steve was waiting for him. Steve could tell by the look on his face that something was wrong. Dr. O'Connor came up to Steve and said, "I'm sorry, Dr. Pratt. I did everything I could to save him. There was just too much damage."

Steve was visibly upset, but managed to say, "Would you say that his death was related to abuse?"

"Yes, most definitely, and from the looks of some of the old hematomas, this boy has been abused for years," replied Dr. O'Connor.

Steve asked, "If it comes down to it, would you testify to that in court?"

"Sure," replied Dr. O'Connor.

"Good, because I want somebody to pay for killing this innocent boy," said Steve.

Both doctors shook hands, and Dr. O'Connor went back into the OR, and Steve went back to the ER. When Steve got downstairs, one of his nurses came up to him and said somewhat out of breath, "Dr. Pratt, the boy's father is here and asking about his son."

Steve nodded at his nurse and could feel his anger boiling up. He stormed into the waiting room, and Mr. Simmons stood and Steve said, "Follow me, Mr. Simmons."

Steve took him into an empty exam room. Once the door shut, Steve turned toward Mr. Simmons, and Steve angrily asked, "How are you already out of jail?"

Mr. Simmons replied, "I know what you've been thinking since I first saw you, that you must think I'm some kind of monster, but it wasn't me. It was my wife. I got her help with medication and counseling and I thought it was working but, I was at work this evening and, when I came home, I found Ricky lying on the living room floor, and my wife was sitting catatonic at the kitchen table. She had my son's blood all over her. That's when I called 911."

Steve immediately settled down and said softly, "I'm so sorry, Mr. Simmons, but your son died on the operating table. There was just too much damage."

Mr. Simmons broke down and cried openly. He said through his crying, "I should have taken Ricky out of that house months ago. I didn't think she was capable of killing my son." Mr. Simmons cried harder.

Steve was astonished that it was Mrs. Simmons who had been hurting Ricky. As Steve remembered when they were here before, she seemed to be the submissive one, and he would have bet his job that Mr. Simmons was the abuser, not his wife.

Later that evening Steve told Dave what had happened with Ricky. Dave told him, "More than likely Mr. Simmons would have covered up for his wife, and nothing would have come from your actions except maybe you possibly losing your license and getting sued for slander."

Steve settled down and replied, "Dave, I know you're right, but it's that *what if* that will make Ricky stay with me for a long time."

Steve walked solemnly back down to the ER. Dave could see how much this case was disturbing him, so Dave went down to the ER and found Steve. He was just coming out of a treatment room, and his face and posture echoed just how bad he felt. Dave stopped him in the hallway and asked, "Steve, why don't you come over after work and we can order pizza. My kids haven't seen you for a long time. It'll help you focus on something else besides Ricky. Come on, it'll be fun!"

Steve didn't want to; he wanted to be alone with his misery, but caved to Dave, and Steve said, "Once again, Dave, you've saved me from myself."

"No, I didn't save you. I have faith in you; I just thought you needed some friendly faces for a change. I've wanted to tell you this for a long time now, and this seems to be a good time. You've come full circle. You've become this great emergency room doctor who used to be impulsive and quick to judge. Now you're responsible, and I would trust you with my life; in fact, I have. Since our adventure on the airplane, it's evident to me and to the workers around you that you're a doctor whom I would trust with my life, and for that, I want to thank you."

Steve got red-faced and was slightly embarrassed about what Dave had said. "It's always nice to hear that you're doing a good job. Thanks."

After work, Steve went over to Dave's house, and they ordered pizza. It was a great environment, and it helped Steve put Ricky's case into perspective. All four of them were in a neck and neck battle as they were playing video bowling. Suddenly, a knock came at Dave's front door. Dave checked his watch and looked at Steve and said, "You aren't expecting anybody, are you?"

Steve shook his head and said, "No."

Dave got up and went to the door, turned on the porch light, and opened the door. Dave's jaws almost hit the floor because there in front of him stood the last person he thought he would ever see again. Lydia!